EP.

AMICA

P9-CRU-178

TOUGH HAND

TOUGH HAND

WAYNE D. OVERHOLSER

THORNDIKE
CHIVERS

This Large Print edition is published by Thorndike Press, Waterville, Maine, USA and by BBC Audiobooks Ltd, Bath, England.

Thorndike Press, a part of Gale, Cengage Learning.

LIBRARY OF CONGRESS CATALOGING-IN-PUBLICATION DATA

Overholser, Wayne D., 1906–1996.
   Tough hand / by Wayne D. Overholser.
     p. cm. — (Thorndike Press large print western)
   ISBN-13: 978-1-4104-1352-9 (alk. paper)
   ISBN-10: 1-4104-1352-7 (alk. paper)
   1. Large type books. I. Title.
PS3529.V33T68 2009
813'.54—dc22   2008049069

BRITISH LIBRARY CATALOGUING-IN-PUBLICATION DATA AVAILABLE

Published in 2009 in the U.S. by arrangement with Golden West Literary Agency.

Published in 2009 in the U.K. by arrangement with Golden West Literary Agency.

U.K. Hardcover: 978 1 408 44116 9 (Chivers Large Print)
U.K. Softcover: 978 1 408 44117 6 (Camden Large Print)

Printed in the United States of America
1 2 3 4 5 6 7 13 12 11 10 09

TOUGH HAND

CHAPTER ONE

Her name was Troy Manders, she was twenty-five; her hair and eyes were black, her face as tanned as any cowhand's because she worked like a man, and there were few jobs that, given an equal start, she couldn't do as well as a man or a little better.

She had, on occasion, blacked a man's eye or bloodied a nose, and cursed him because he wouldn't swing on her. She could draw her .38 and spill five slugs before you could figure out how she filled her hand so fast, and if she was showing off she'd make a tin can jump with every bullet. The only thing she couldn't do was to break a wild horse. That was why she'd given Jim Sullivan a job. As for him, she'd fascinated him from the first time he'd heard about her. That was why he took the job.

She ruled a crew of nine men with an iron hand. Eight of them, from the cook, old Longhorn Flannigan, on down to the tough

Dykens boys, followed her with a blind loyalty they would never have given a man. The ninth was Jim, who figured she had a soft side, and he tagged along on the off chance that some day he'd get a look at it. He did, the night they camped on the Dolores River, two days' drive from Rampart Valley.

They had driven a cow-and-calf herd from the Dry Cimarron across the range to the Dolores, and nobody in the outfit except Troy had known where they were headed or why. She'd said they were driving west, and that had been enough for everybody but Jim, who studied her the way any man would who possessed an overgrown bump of curiosity.

She had baffled Jim from the first. She still did, but she had changed. For the last week he had sensed a growing nervous tension in her. Nervousness was as peculiar to her as she was peculiar to the entire female half of the human race.

She had ridden point most of the time since they'd left the Cimarron, usually with Gabe Dykens, who could find his way out of a cave blindfolded, but after they'd hit the Las Animas at Durango she had ordered Jim to ride point, and Gabe went back to eat the dust of the drag. Obviously she was

8

in familiar country.

Now, with the herd bedded down and the moon showing above the San Juan range to the east, she was as nervous as a cat that had been running with a pack of hounds and suddenly discovered she was different.

She borrowed the makings from Jim and rolled a cigarette, her fingers awkward with the paper because she seldom smoked. Jim had it figured she needed a cigarette now to prove to herself she was equal to any man in the outfit. But it didn't quite add up, because she had never needed such assurance before. Jim decided there must be something else, but he didn't have the foggiest notion what it was.

She handed the makings back and lighted the cigarette with a cedar twig from the campfire. She put her hands on her hips, the cigarette dangling from one corner of her mouth, and said, "Come here." They obeyed, and all of them, even Moloch Dykens, who was kill-crazy and not too bright, seemed to sense that something was up.

"Boys," Troy said, "I guess nobody ever had a better crew. We've been through a lot, but it isn't a patching to what's ahead if we stay together, so if any of you want your time I'll pay you off and no questions asked.

No hard feelings, either."

They had been through a lot together, and no mistake. Troy's ranch had been in No Man's Land where law was conspicuous by its absence, and if you weren't tougher than your neighbors you wound up looking at the stars but not seeing them because you had a bullet between your eyes.

But for Troy to talk that way just wasn't natural. They looked at her, as stunned as if she'd taken a singletree from the hooligan wagon and hit each of them over the head. Jim was the first to recover. He said: "You're talking crazy, Troy. Nobody wants his time."

"That's right," Gabe Dykens said. "You say to put this herd on top of Pike's Peak, and we'll sure as hell get 'em there."

Moloch Dykens bobbed his head. Moloch was the damnedest name for a man Jim had ever heard, but the youngest Dykens boy's mother must have been inspired. The name fitted him like the hair on your head. He always had a fatuous smile on his face that turned out to be a horrible grimace because his lips never came together. Two of his upper front teeth were missing, and he kept the tip of his tongue stuck up there where the teeth should have been. He wanted two things out of life: a full belly at meal time and a chance to kill a man now and then.

He'd been happy ever since he'd signed on with Troy.

"You want some hombre rubbed out, maybe, ma'am?" Moloch asked hopefully.

"No." Troy threw her cigarette into the fire as if she had suddenly realized she didn't need it. "We're taking this herd to Rampart Valley and we're throwing it on a piece of grass that was stolen from my father nine years ago. A section of land with the buildings still belongs to me, but the minute we show up we've got trouble. I want all of you to know what we're heading into."

Enoch Dykens, the middle brother, who was the biggest of the three and who always reminded Jim of a Labrador pup, said, "Ma'am, when we back off from trouble, I hope the good Lord strikes us dead, I sure do."

And Jim: "So we're going to have trouble. All right, Troy, just tell us what to do."

She gave Jim a grateful glance. If there was a leader among the men, it was Jim Sullivan. When Troy wasn't around, all the others except the Dykens boys instinctively looked to him for orders. No one felt any resentment except Gabe Dykens, who had some notions of his own about Troy but had never got around to mentioning them to her.

"It's going to take some scheming," Troy

11

said, "because we're up against a two-headed proposition. One of them is a big-bellied range bully, named Nate Pollock, who has the largest spread in the valley. The other one's a smooth-talking banker named Matt Seery. Pollock can he handled, but Seery's going to be tough."

"His hide ain't so tough it'll stop a .45 slug," Moloch said, still hopeful.

"No killing unless we're shoved into it," Troy said sternly. "You understand that, Molly?"

"He's just talking," Gabe said.

"It's up to you to see that he is. Now then. We're two days' drive from Rampart Valley. We'll leave the river here and swing north so we'll come into the valley from the east. I aim to drive through town so everybody, including Matt Seery, will know Troy Manders is back. Gabe, I've got a job for you and Enoch and Moloch. You listening?"

Gabe was a tall, lantern-jawed man with abnormally long ears that were sharply pointed. He wasn't proud of his ears, and he'd almost beaten Baldy Cronin to death when Baldy had called him "Jackass Dykens." No one had used the name since.

Gabe grinned and nodded. "I'm all ears, Troy."

His brother Enoch laughed. "We can see

12

that." Enoch, bigger than Gabe, could safely needle him when no one else could.

"You boys start out in the morning, but you won't come with the rest of us," Troy said. "You'll head straight for Bakeoven, which is the only town in Rampart Valley. I said head for it, not go there. When you get to Starlight Mesa, which is just south of the valley, you'll start looking for Seery's cow camp. He'll have three or four hands up there, and this time of year he'll be rounding up his beef herd to drive them down to the valley. Be sure it's Seery's outfit. His iron is the Horseshoe Bar. Burn the cabin and scatter his gather and throw the fear of God into his men. Don't let them get a good look at you. I don't want the law on your tail."

Gabe nodded, frowning. "I thought this Seery hombre was a banker."

"He is, but he has a little spread just north of my place. He plays around with his ranch like he does some other things, but banking is his main business. Hide out two or three days, then hunt us up. My old iron was the Triangle M. My buildings are at the west end of the valley at the foot of Telescope Mountain. If you can't find it, ask."

"We'll find it," Gabe said.

She turned to Jim. "You'll ride with them

for about ten miles, but when you reach the mesa you'll leave them. Head north and go into Bakeoven. Don't let on you have anything to do with us. If the rest of you boys see Jim when we get to town, pretend you don't know him." She dug into her pocket and gave Jim a handful of gold coins. "Buy a store suit. Get the best room in the hotel. You're going to be a promoter."

Old Longhorn Flannigan guffawed. "Promoter, is it? The only thing he ever promoted was a poker game."

"It's all right if he does that, too," Troy said quickly, "but it isn't all he'll promote. I'm gambling on Jim's brain. I think he can outsmart Seery any day in the week."

"Looks to me like you're playing more'n one string on your fiddle," Baldy Cronin said.

"That's right," Troy agreed. "I've been figuring how to play this fiddle ever since I left the valley nine years ago." She looked around the circle of men, confident now, her nervousness gone, then she pinned her eyes on Jim and jerked her head toward the river. She said, in the imperious way she had when she wanted to be obeyed at once, "You and me are taking a walk."

She wheeled and strode away. Jim hesitated, his gaze meeting Gabe Dykens', and

14

he saw the wild, jealous hatred that was in the man's pale eyes. If Jim remained with Troy, he'd have to kill Gabe. Maybe his brothers, too. But this wasn't the day.

"Some other time, Gabe," Jim said, and followed Troy.

CHAPTER TWO

He caught Troy before she reached the river, and walked downstream with her, the moon a round, reddish ball behind them. The river had not been hard to cross at that point; it was wide and shallow, a chocolate-colored stream that was momentarily sluggish before it plunged into a narrow, high-walled canyon. Even from where they stood, Jim could hear its distant rumble as it boomed through the gorge.

Troy took his arm. Her hand trembled a little, and he felt tension in her again. He wondered why she had gripped his arm. She had never touched him before. Their relationship had been strictly that of man with man.

She was the only woman he had ever known who apparently had no interest in romance. She'd always given him the impression she'd use her gun on the first man who made love to her. That was one reason she fascinated Jim.

He wasn't sure he had ever seen the real Troy Manders. He understood she had used the only method she could to hold off men like Gabe Dykens. She needed him and his brothers, but if she hadn't held him at arm's length she'd have been forced to fire him a long time ago.

Troy halted when she reached a small sandy beach between the screen of willows and the river. She said, "Here," and sat down. He dropped into the sand beside her. She had released his arm, but now she bent toward him so that he could feel the point of her shoulder.

"You're wondering, aren't you?" she asked.

"A little."

"More than a little, I guess." She picked up a rock and tossed it into the water that made a black, forbidding shine in the moonlight. "You've been with me one year, two months, two weeks, and three days. Remember how it started?"

This was a night of surprises. He'd had no idea she had counted the days since she had hired him. He said: "I remember, all right. I was breaking some horses in Clayton. You happened to be in town, and you watched me ride that black gelding they

17

called Big Devil."

She laughed softly. "Ah, that was a ride, man. I bought the horse and hired you. Why did you take my offer?"

It was a hard question to answer. He couldn't say he'd been curious because he'd heard fabulous talk about her and about the salty crew she held together and the way she'd run a ranch over there in No Man's Land where more than one tough cowman had been whipped by predatory neighbors. He'd fix things up fine if he told her he'd wanted to study her as a scientist examines an unusual specimen.

He said finally: "It was a good offer. More money than I was making."

"Don't lie to me, Jim," she said quietly.

"Well, I guess I wanted to see what you were like," he said lamely. "I'd heard there wasn't anyone else in the world like Troy Manders."

She studied his words a moment, then said: "I suppose that could be the truth. Jim, after all this time I don't know you. Oh, I can see you're six feet tall and you weigh maybe one seventy-five. You've got red hair and blue eyes and a nose that isn't pretty because it's cocked over to one side like somebody had put it there with a fist. I know you're fast with a gun and you can

18

use your fists. You can lick Gabe Dykens if you have to."

He wasn't too sure. He said, "Troy, if you're going to stay in Rampart Valley, you'll have to fire the Dykens boys."

"I can't, and don't get me off the subject. I've told you what I can see. Now I've got to know the rest of it. Who are you, Jim?"

"A bronc buster who was making a slim living when you picked me up and gave me a job."

"You're ducking," she said impatiently. "I'm not just quizzing: I have a reason for asking. Where did you come from? What have you done?"

He was silent for a moment, wondering what he could tell her. He was twenty-seven, and he hadn't done much of anything that counted. He'd spent the last eight years exploring life, but nothing had panned out. He remembered how it had been when he left home, so sure of himself, so certain there was nothing on God's earth he couldn't do. Well, maybe he'd proved he was right, but what had it got him?

She laid a hand on his leg, her shoulder still pressed against his. "Tell me, Jim," she said.

"I was born on a ranch on the South Platte," he said. "I went to school. Even had

19

a year of college. Left home when I was nineteen and I've never gone back."

He stopped, thinking about his folks, good people, solid people who had worked hard and were probably still working hard. They had loved him, he guessed, if people who put great store in cattle and land and money in the bank ever really loved anyone. But they hadn't understood that he was a natural rebel who resented having his life decided for him, that he was the kind who just had to get out and see what made the world go round. So he'd saddled up one day and started out, and he'd been going ever since.

"Go on." Her grip tightened. "Go on, Jim."

"Not much else to tell," he said wearily. "I've always had a hell of a curiosity about things and people. I tried my hand at every job that came along. Stage driving. Mining. Taught school one winter in South Park. Worked on a newspaper in Leadville. Cut ties. Put up hay." He grinned. "I even tried breaking horses. Remember?"

She was in no mood for levity. She probed his past with another question. "You never held any other job as long as you did this one. That right?"

"That's right."

"Why have you stayed?"

He couldn't keep on ducking the question. He might just as well answer it. He said, "I've been trying to figure you out, and I'm still trying."

She took a long breath, her hand inching upward along his thigh, her fingers gripping so tightly they hurt. "Now you're being honest. I guess I knew all the time that I've been some sort of crazy freak to you." She took another long breath, and added, "Troy Manders, who was born a woman and has been trying to prove the Creator wrong ever since."

He was silent, uneasy. He had always thought she possessed a soft streak, and he wondered if she was going to show it now.

"I've got to tell you about me," she said, "so you can do what I want done in Bakeoven. There was just my father and me on the Triangle M. My mother died when I was small. My father wanted a boy, and I suppose he raised me like one, but I was just a girl until it happened. Matt Seery wanted our place, but Dad wouldn't sell. Then Nate Pollock got ornery.

"Afterwards I figured out he belonged to Seery, but I don't suppose anyone else would believe that. Everybody thinks Seery's God, or mighty near it. Anyhow, Pollock's bunch rode in one night and shot Dad. One of them knocked me out. When I came to, they were gone."

"Did you go to the sheriff?"

"The county seat's a long ways from Bakeoven, but we had a deputy. When I talked to him, he laughed in my face. Said it was outlaws who came down from Telescope Mountain. So I took Dad's money and left. It was quite a bit. He kept it buried in the cellar because he didn't trust Seery's bank. I used it to get a start, and I've been lucky."

She withdrew her hand and lay back, staring up at the sky. "I used to wake up screaming, thinking about that night. Dad was a kind man. Read a lot. He used to say that vengeance was the Lord's and that a man sinned if he tried to square up for something like this. I hope he was wrong, because ever since then I've thought about how I would go back and destroy Pollock and Matt Seery. Now I'm going to do it."

Jim lay back, his hands under his head. So that was it. Nine years of hating and thinking about revenge had made Troy Manders the woman he knew, living like a man, thinking like a man, molding herself into the kind of woman who could do a man's job. For the first time since he had known her, he was sorry for her, but he couldn't

22

tell her so. Whatever she wanted from others, it wasn't sympathy.

"Your father wasn't wrong," he said. "You are. Don't go ahead with it."

"I didn't expect you to say that," she said in a low tone. "I've told you this because I want you to do a special thing. I thought you'd understand, but I expected too much."

He raised himself on one shoulder and looked at her. She did not move. The moonlight fell on her face and on the dark hair she wore pinned tightly at the back of her head. A perfectly shaped nose. A strong chin. A full-lipped mouth that on another woman would have indicated great depth of passion. He had never really looked at her before. Not the way he was looking now. She could be pretty.

He said: "I'll do what you want done, but I still say you're wrong. You're a woman."

"Sure, I should get married," she said dully, "and have a lot of children. I'd like to, Jim, but this thing comes first."

"What do you want me to do?"

"I told you part of it a while ago. The rest of it is to get acquainted with Seery. Pretend you're an engineer and you represent a lot of money. You can fool him, all right. Tell him you've heard about Rampart Valley. A creek comes through my place. I have a natural reservoir site. Try to buy my place. See what he says."

"If you get him interested in bringing in settlers and developing an irrigation project, you'll throw him against the rest of the valley. That what you're working for?"

"That's it. I have a great deal of money, and I'll use all I need of it to suck him into the deal." She was silent a moment, her eyes on the stars, her hands fisted at her sides in the sand. Finally she said: "Jim, it makes me crazy mad when I think how the Seerys pretend to be such good people. Alexander Seery — that's Matt's father — founded the town of Bakeoven. And his mother, well, you'd think she was an angel flapping her wings in your face."

"Suppose he offers to buy your ranch for a good price?"

"I'd sell," she answered quickly, "but I'll stay in the valley until Matt Seery crawls out of it on his belly."

Jim lay back on the sand. "Why do you want his herd busted up?"

"Two reasons. One is to make him mad. The other is to make him listen to your proposition. He'll lose a month getting his beef herd to the railroad. Maybe more if we have an early storm. He'll miss the top price, and his steers will be mighty lank by the time he gets them to Denver. I'm gambling he'll be so sick of the stock business he'll jump at your offer."

It was a good plan, Jim thought, about as cold-blooded as anything he had heard. He was silent for several minutes, considering what his part in it would be. The job didn't appeal to him, but he'd go along just to find out what happened to Troy.

Suddenly, without warning, she sat up and moved toward him. She put her hands palm down against the sand, his head between them. Then, with her body over his, she lowered her face and kissed him, her breasts pressed against his chest. His first reaction was shocked surprise; then he was stirred by her, and his arms came around her and he held her hard against him.

She pulled away, one hand caressing his stubble-covered cheek. "You need a shave." She laughed shakily. "Jim, that was the first time I've kissed a man since I was sixteen, and I didn't aim to now. I just got to thinking that it won't ever be the same again, having you around and seeing you every day. I wish I could look ahead."

"I'll be around," he said, and tried to draw her back to him, but she wrenched free from his arms and got to her feet.

"Let's go back to camp," she said.

This time she did not take his arm. He wondered if she had wanted to kiss him all this time and had been held back because she had known she'd have to back away from what she was determined to do. He sensed that she was scared, maybe because she was close to Rampart Valley and her father's teachings were coming back to her again.

She had let Jim see into her soul tonight. In the morning she might regret it. Well, she had her soft side, all right, but she had carefully hidden it for nine years. Perhaps she had even hidden it from herself.

Jim shared a night-herd shift with Gabe Dykens. Before they rode out of camp, Gabe said, "I didn't like you going off with Troy tonight."

"She gave me an order," Jim said.

"I heard. Well, you may be a smart hombre, but you ain't much man, not by my figuring. Maybe you've fooled her on account of she can't bust a bad horse and you can."

"Nobody fools Troy," Jim said. "Not even you."

"I'll make this plain." Gabe's voice was sharply honed by frustration. "She's mine.

She don't know it yet, but she will."

"You ought to know I don't bluff," Jim said. "If you want me out of the way, you'd better have Moloch shoot me in the back."

"Good idea," Gabe said, and rode away.

Jim mounted his roan gelding, then hesitated, eyes on the campfire that was a small red spot in the blanketing darkness. Troy was sleeping there. He remembered how she had felt in his arms and how he had wanted her with a savage desire that had never been in him before.

In all the time he had worked for Troy, he had not given much thought to her as a woman a man could love, but she wanted him to think of her that way, or she wouldn't have kissed him. She was a woman, a lot of woman. Tonight he had lost a chance he might never have again. Sick with regret, he rode up the slope to the sagebrush flat where the herd was bedded down.

CHAPTER THREE

Jim wondered whether Troy would be any different at breakfast than she had always been, but he soon found out that what had happened last night might just as well not have happened at all. He knew that if he said anything in front of the crew about kissing her, she'd have no choice except to hit him on the mouth and call him a damned liar.

Jim was sure of one thing. Gabe Dykens had no doubt about what had taken place last night along the river. Every time Jim glanced at the man, he saw the ugly suspicion that lay festering in Gabe's mind. Jim wouldn't give either Gabe or Moloch his back today.

Troy had only one thing to say before Jim left with the Dykens boys, and when she spoke her voice was coolly impersonal. "I expect to drive through Bakeoven about ten o'clock day after tomorrow. I want you to be on the street. If you can manage it, have Matt Seery with you."

"I'll see what I can do," Jim said, keeping his voice as impersonal as Troy's.

He rode northwest from camp, taking the lead until they topped a cedar-covered ridge, then he reined up and looked back. Moloch was staring at him with fixed intensity, his meaty lips parted, the tip of his tongue protruding through the gap in his front teeth.

Jim's right hand dropped to his gun butt. He said, "Molly, if you're fixing to plug me, go ahead and get it over with."

Jim knew he couldn't beat all three of them if it came to a shootout, but he could get Gabe and maybe Moloch, and he thought Gabe knew it. Apparently Moloch had his orders, for now he threw Gabe a questioning glance.

"We'll wait," Gabe said.

"If I don't show up in Bakeoven, Troy's little scheme will be knocked in the head," Jim said. "How do you think she's going to like that?"

"What makes you think we're fixing to beef you?" Gabe asked, his lean face showing curiosity.

"It's written all over your ugly mug," Jim said. "You know I'm faster than you are and you don't want to die, so I figure you aim for Moloch to give it to me in the back."

"Naw, we'll give you an even break." Enoch laughed. "That good enough, Jim?"

"That's all I want," Jim said, "but I doubt that Gabe's as fair-minded as you are."

If it wasn't for Gabe's dominance, Jim thought, Enoch would be a run-of-the-mill, hard-working cowhand. Now, however, he was as dangerous as either of his brothers. For a moment no one moved, Gabe considering his chances and not liking them.

"No hurry," Gabe said finally.

"I figure there is," Jim said. "I can't always watch my back."

Gabe motioned with his left hand. "Start riding. We've got work to do."

Jim sat his saddle, doggedly stubborn. "I've only got one life and I like it. I'll eat your dust."

Gabe shrugged. "Suits me. I ain't one to eat another man's dust anyhow."

He rode past, Moloch reining in beside him. Enoch hesitated, laughing again. He was a great hand for laughing, especially when he got into a fight and had his hands on another man's throat. The lust to kill was in all of them, although Enoch required a little pushing to make him fight. Gabe had a sly and careful mind that always considered the odds before he made a move. Moloch was the worst of the three because he had no inhibitions, and he wasn't smart enough to be scared. He'd have been killed years ago if Gabe hadn't looked out for him.

"You're a smart huckleberry," Enoch said. "Too smart for me. Ever since you signed on with Troy, I've been trying to figure out what your game was, but I can't catch it. Maybe you've just been waiting for what you got last night."

It would be of no use for Jim to say he hadn't "got" anything. Enoch wouldn't believe him. Or if he did, he'd lose all his respect for Jim. To Enoch's way of thinking, a man would be no man at all if he went walking along a riverbank with a woman and was satisfied with a kiss.

"Maybe," Jim said, and let it go at that.

Enoch grinned knowingly, winked, and caught up with his brothers. Jim followed, keeping twenty feet or more behind them. They dropped down the north side of the ridge and climbed another, and then another. The spiny hogbacks were as much alike as .45 shells in a man's cartridge belt, dry and covered with red boulders. Not much vegetation, just cactus and yucca and a few runty cedars. Hard-scrabble range for sure.

Jim, keeping his eyes on the men ahead, thought about the way in which Troy had gathered her crew. He was the last to sign on, but he'd heard about the others. Longhorn Flannigan had been the first. He'd been with a caravan headed for Santa Fe when he'd taken down with scarlet fever. They had left him beside the trail to die. Troy had found him, taken him home, and nursed him back to health.

Baldy Cronin's horse had hit a badger hole and broken a leg. Baldy had been out of his head and close to dying of thirst when Troy had found him and saved his life. Joe Morgan had shot a man in Dodge City, and Troy had given him a place to hide out until they'd heard the shooting had been termed justifiable homicide. Joe stayed on, allowing he'd have been running the rest of his life if it hadn't been for Troy.

It had gone that way with the others until Troy had got the Dykens boys. The way Jim had heard the story from Flannigan, it was the only foolish thing she'd done, but even it had panned out all right.

A stage had been held up in New Mexico and the driver murdered. The sheriff had surprised the Dykens boys looking the body over and had taken them to jail. That night a lynch mob broke into their cell and would have swung them if Troy and her crew hadn't spoiled the party and got the Dykens boys out of town.

According to Flannigan, there had been some grumbling about it among Troy's old hands, mostly because they weren't sure who was guilty. Later on, the sheriff had found the right parties and they'd been convicted. That had put the Dykens boys in the clear, and it had made Troy look good.

"She had the right hunch," old Longhorn admitted, "but how in hell she knew I couldn't guess."

Just luck, Jim had always thought. Better to be born lucky than rich, he had heard someone say. Whether Troy's luck would hold in Rampart Valley was another question. Jim was the only man in the crew who didn't owe a mile-high debt to Troy, and that put him in a class apart from the rest. The chances were that every man in the outfit had the same suspicion about last night that Gabe had.

Jim hadn't given it a thought that morning when they'd eaten breakfast; he'd been thinking of Troy and watching Gabe at the same time. But he had time to think about it now, and the more he thought, the more he realized it was a bad deal. Troy should have known it.

The other men would hate him, even old Longhorn, who had been his best friend. But maybe Troy had foreseen it. Maybe it was the reason she had said it would never be the same again. It wouldn't, either. He wished, as Troy had, that he could look ahead.

Somewhere near midmorning they climbed a steep, rock-strewn hill and found themselves on a level mesa that apparently ran on for miles. Gabe pulled up and waited for Jim to reach him.

"You figure this is what Troy called Starlight Mesa?" Gabe asked.

"Looks like it," Jim answered.

Gabe nodded as if he had decided the same thing. "Reckon we've gone ten miles?"

"Just about."

"Then this is where you head for town," Gabe said. "We'll start looking for Seery's cow camp."

It was easier than Jim had thought. Gabe rode directly west along the edge of the mesa hill, Enoch and Moloch following. Jim waited until they disappeared into a forest of close-growing piñons. Suddenly it struck him that it was too easy. He cracked steel to his roan, swinging northward across an open area a mile or more in width. They might circle on him, but at least he had put some distance between him and them.

He crashed through a thicket of service-berry brush and came into another grass-covered meadow, an annoying prickle along his spine. Ten minutes later he reached a dark wall of piñon and felt easier when it closed behind him.

Reining up, he sat his saddle for a minute or more listening, but he heard nothing except the thin sound of the wind in the piñons. Boogery, he told himself, but he knew Moloch. The fellow might slip away to do a job he knew Gabe wanted done.

Moloch looked upon his older brother much as a lonesome hound looks upon its master. The cuffings Gabe gave him when he got out of line did not detract from Moloch's unswerving loyalty. It was different with Enoch. At times Jim had the feeling Moloch hated Enoch.

The sun was noon high when Jim reached the north rim of the mesa and looked down into Rampart Valley. It was five to eight miles wide and maybe forty miles long, he judged, running east and west, with the Dolores River cutting it in half. The river disappeared to the north, slashing another narrow gorge through the red sandstone, and rolling on to flow eventually into the Colorado.

The drop below Jim was sheer, five hundred feet or more. He could see the town of Bakeoven on the other side of the river, a huddle of buildings made hazy by distance. At this point it was hard to judge the number of miles, but it might as well have been a thousand if he didn't find a trail that led from the mesa to the valley floor.

Jim debated which way to go. If he turned east, he would be putting more miles between him and Bakeoven, and he had to be there before the stores closed if he was to buy the clothes Troy had told him to get. Besides, he needed a bath and a shave. He squinted at the sun, estimating his time, and decided to ride west. There must be a trail from the rim to the valley floor if Matt Seery summered his herd on the mesa.

It was hard going, fighting his way through jungles of scrub oak or picking a path across barren stretches of spiny red sandstone ridges covered by grotesque obelisks and arches. Then, in midafternoon, he discovered a trail that followed a narrow break in the slickrock rim. Half an hour later he was on the valley floor, which was sparsely covered by grama grass and shad scale. If this was typical of Rampart Valley, he wondered how so many people found a living in it.

He reined up to let his roan blow for a couple of minutes, then swung westward toward the river, realizing that the valley was longer than he had first thought. Ahead of him, twenty miles away or more, was Telescope Mountain, a three-headed peak, its shoulders covered by quaking aspens. Above them long fingers of spruce, turned blue by distance, reached to timber line. Here and there a few spots of snow clung to the bottoms of deep, constantly shaded canyons near the top of the mountain.

Time was running out, but he didn't press his tired horse. An hour later he reached the Dolores, a bridge spanning it near the south side of the valley. Bakeoven lay directly ahead of him on the west bank of the river.

He rode into town slowly, wanting to attract as little attention as possible. Main Street was covered with red dust hock-deep, the short business block flanked by the usual false fronts. There was one exception, and it was this that struck Jim at once, setting Bakeoven apart from any of a hundred similar cow towns he had seen.

A two-story granite building stood in the middle of the frame structures on the north side of the street. As Jim rode past, he saw the tall black letters, BAKEOVEN, STATE

BANK, MATTHEW SEERY, PRES.

So it was Matt Seery's town, just as Troy had said. The grim strength and air of permanence that the stone building possessed seemed to prove the point. Jim judged that it had been designed to stand as a symbol of Seery's strength and position.

For the first time Jim began to doubt Troy's wisdom in sending him on what could be a fool's errand. Probably Seery had everything he wanted right there in Bakeoven. If he did, he would have nothing to do with a fake irrigation scheme.

Jim found a livery stable at the end of the block. He stripped gear from his roan, rubbed him down, and told the stableman, "Grain him double." The hostler looked at the gelding and nodded. The horse showed the hard ride that was behind him. As Jim left the stable, he felt the man's curious eyes on him. Strangers were probably not common in Bakeoven.

A general store was still open. Jim bought the best suit in the place, a brown broadcloth that fitted him as well as he could expect, although the coat was a little tight on his broad shoulders. He judged it had been hanging there a long time. The storekeeper, a bent-shouldered old man with a

38

skimpy white beard, went into a long harangue to the effect that Jim would find no better material in the county.

Jim bought a white shirt, socks, underclothes, a string tie, and a black derby. He paid in gold, ignoring the obvious curiosity of the old man, and gathering up his purchases, left the store. As he crossed the street to the barbershop, he saw two riders coming into town from the west. Otherwise the street was deserted.

Something was wrong. At that time of day, there should be people on the street, at least some of the townsmen who would be going home to supper. Jim glanced briefly at the horsemen, who were about fifty feet from him, and hurried on, afraid the barbershop would be closed before he got there.

He made the high step to the walk, crossed to the door of the shop, and asked, "You going to be open long enough for me to get a shave and a bath?"

The barber was alone, a small, pink-cheeked man who was absent-mindedly stropping a razor. He was scowling and talking to himself in an argumentative tone, as if trying to convince himself of something he didn't believe. Again the feeling rose in Jim that trouble was brewing.

"Didn't you hear me? I said I wanted a

bath and a shave." Jim's voice was clipped, harsh.

The barber jumped and looked up, the razor motionless in midair above the strap. "Sorry. Didn't know you were there." He glanced at the clothes in Jim's hands; his eyes swung to the gun on Jim's hip, and he hesitated, his gaze lingering on the cowhand's face. He seemed momentarily caught in a bog of mental indecision, then he said: "Come in. I've got a fire going, and there's a boiler of water heating now. Be a little while, though."

"You can give me a shave while it's heating," Jim said.

The barber nodded absently and went on stropping his razor. The door into the bathroom was open. Jim went through it, the heat from the big range rushing at him. He laid the clothes on a bench, stoked up the fire, and tested the water in the copper boiler. Lukewarm now, but it would be hot by the time he had his shave. The zinc tub had not been used for a few days, and it was covered with a layer of red dust. Jim dipped some of the water into the tub and washed it out.

Someone came in. Jim remained on his knees, his head turned to listen. A man said: "The stage won't leave for two, three hours.

What are you going to do, Marshal?"

"Not a damn' thing," the barber shouted defensively. "Bob Jarvis and the girl knew they couldn't make it."

"Your job is to keep the peace," the other man said. "How long are you going to let Nate Pollock run rough-shod over this town?"

"I don't know," the barber snapped. "But by God, I know one thing. You can have my star right now. I'm not a lawman. I'm a barber."

"You're all the lawman we've got," the other said, his tone doggedly stubborn. "I don't want your star. I just want you to see that Pollock's toughs don't get out of hand."

Jim rose and stepped to the door in time to see the barber yank a drawer open, take out a star, and throw it at the man standing in the doorway. "I'm resigning as of now," the barber shouted. "Why I ever took the star I don't know, but I do know I wasn't hired to buck Nate Pollock."

The man in the doorway slipped the star into his pocket. There seemed to be nothing outstanding about him, an average-tall, unassuming man with white hair and a closely cropped mustache as white as his hair. A townsman, probably the owner of some business on Main Street.

"I'm just the mayor," the man in the doorway said, "but I wish I was the council. Then I'd see there was money enough in the treasury to hire a gun-fighting marshal and not a scissors snipper." He wheeled and walked away.

The barber was white-faced and trembling. He kept on stropping the razor as Jim sat down in the chair. It was a long moment before he turned, shook out a white cloth, and pinned it around Jim's neck. He asked, "Stranger?"

"You know I am," Jim said. "I don't cotton to having a shaky man shave me. My throat cuts easy."

The barber gave him a sickly grin. "I'm not shaky, but you will be before you get that bath."

Turning, he picked up a mug and brush and immediately put them down. Jim said, "I don't savvy."

"You will. Just sit right there, friend. I'll get some hot water."

The barber hurried into the bathroom. Jim leaned back, weary from the long ride, and grinned wryly as he considered his bad luck in hitting Bakeoven at a time when trouble with which he had nothing to do was obviously coming into sharp and deadly focus.

His eyes idly ran along the shelves at one end of the mirror where the private shaving mugs belonging to the regular customers stood, their names printed on one side in ornate gold letters. He read "Jess Darket" on the first mug on the top shelf, his gaze swinging along the line of mugs until it came to "Matt Seery."

He laughed softly, for he was seeing exactly what he thought he would see. Seery's mug was by far the biggest of the entire collection, and the gold letters on it were taller and more ornate than the others. On this range Seery must be quite a man, Jim thought, quite a man.

CHAPTER FOUR

The barber was gone only a minute or two, and when he returned color had flowed back into his cheeks and he wasn't trembling. When he began lathering Jim's face, he was close enough for Jim to smell the whisky.

"What's this all about?" Jim asked.

"You have no idea, friend." The barber dipped a cloth into a pan of water, gave it a quick twist, and laid it on Jim's face. "What you don't know won't hurt you."

That was true, Jim thought. The question had been a mistake. His immediate business was with Matt Seery. But one thing seemed plain enough. It was Pollock, not Seery, who had a tight cinch on the country. Well, nine years was long enough for a lot of things to change. Troy would find that out.

The barber worked fast, too fast, it seemed to Jim. He acted as if he wanted to get the job over and done with. He had finished and was rubbing cologne on Jim's face when the reason for his anxiety became plain. A man came in from the street. Jim heard the barber's quick intake of breath as he snatched the cloth away from the back of Jim's neck and gave it a vigorous shake.

"Howdy, Bert," the barber said, uneasily.

The fellow was one of the two who had been riding into town when Jim had crossed the street. He was tall and rail-thin, with a long red neck and a droopy yellow mustache. His eyes were small and black and beady. He wasn't a handsome man by any standard except his own. Shiny spike-heeled boots, expensive white Stetson, a pearl-handled Colt in a low-hung holster, and a black-and-white calf-skin vest: all pointed to an exaggerated vanity.

He glanced first at his mirrored image, ignoring Jim and the barber as he teetered back and forth on his heels. Then, satisfied with what he saw, he brought his gaze to the barber, asking, "Got some hot water, Ed?"

"Why yes," the barber said, "but this fellow here has already asked for the tub."

Jim rose and stepped away from the chair. He said, "Looks like you're next, mister."

As Jim watched a slow grin crawl across

45

the other's arrogant face, he knew that on a range like this, where one spread carried all the weight, every cowhand who rode for that outfit figured he was a little tougher than the next man — and maybe he was, or he didn't keep his job. But right now Jim held one advantage. He was a stranger.

"I'm Bert Knoll," the cowboy said, as if the name should mean something. "I never wait for a bath if the water's hot. The other gent waits."

"I'm Jim Sullivan," Jim said, his voice matching Knoll's tone. "It's some other gent who waits, not me. I never killed a man for a tub of hot water, but I would."

Knoll began to swell like a pigeon, his neck redder than it had been. He said to the barber: "You know I ain't a patient man, Maylor. Get this huckleberry out of here."

"It's your chore, Bert," the barber said. "You tend to it."

"By God, I will," Knoll shouted. "This is the damnedest thing I ever heard of, trying to make me wait. Me'n Perkins came to town to do a job, Maylor, and I ain't got time to wait."

"I know," the barber murmured. "Two of you ought to be able to take care of young Jarvis."

"We figure we can," Knoll agreed, "but

we ain't had supper yet. By the time Perkins and me eat, the stage'll be due out of town, and I ain't got time to wait for no lousy cowhand to scrape the dirt off."

Knoll started toward the bathroom, swaggering a little, as if he had no doubt he had established his right to the bath. He had taken two steps when Jim drew his gun. He said, "Mister, you walk through that bathroom door and I will have killed a man for a tub of hot water."

Knoll swung around, his right hand splayed over his gun butt, but he didn't draw. He looked at the Colt in Jim's hands, obviously astounded by the fact that a stranger had the temerity to pull a gun on him. At last he spoke, but his voice was soft, almost toneless, as he said: "Looks like you're holding the big ace. All right, take your bath and be damned, but get one thing straight: you'll be leaving on the next stage."

"Not me," Jim said. "I have business here, and I'll stay till I get done with it." He swung his gun to keep it on Knoll as the man walked out. Then he laughed, and asked, "Am I shaking, Mr. Maylor?"

Knoll went on into the street and disappeared. The barber said: "Take a good bath, friend. A clean corpse is nice to handle. I don't get many in this country."

"You the undertaker?"

"That's right."

"Then you'll be handling a dirty corpse."

"Two of 'em, if it ain't you."

"I'm generous. I'll see you get two of them."

Jim winked at the barber, and going into the bathroom, closed the door and gave the turnpin a twist. He poured the boiler of hot water into the zinc tub, picked up a bucket, went out through the back, and filled it at the pump. It took three buckets to cool the water, then he locked the back door and took off his clothes. He placed his gun on a bench, shoved it to the head of the tub, and got in.

For a long time he lay there, eyes closed, finding relaxation for nerves and tired muscles. But now, with time to think, he wasn't sure he had done the right thing. Getting into a gun fight with a couple of hired toughs wasn't doing the job Troy had sent him to do.

Jim had no illusions about his faults. He was particularly aware of two of them: driving curiosity, and an instinctive stubbornness when someone began pushing him. The first had caused him to wander restlessly for years and then, strangely enough, had roped him to his job with Troy. The

48

second had made him leave home. Because his folks had planned his future for him, he had wanted no part of it.

Well, he had got his nose caught in a mouse trap for sure this time. It wasn't so much that he was afraid of Knoll or of his partner. The thing was that an outfit like Nate Pollock's mounted a bad reputation and then was forced to stick with it. The chances were it had been years since one of Pollock's hands had been called. Now he'd probably have the whole outfit on his neck just to keep its reputation untarnished.

Another angle worried Jim. What would Matt Seery's reaction be when he heard that Jim had stood up to a Pollock man? It was a question Jim couldn't answer until he knew more about the relationship between Pollock and Seery. Troy had guessed Pollock belonged to Seery, but she might have been wrong, or the situation might have changed in nine years.

Jim got out of the tub and dried himself with a rough towel he found hanging on a nail. No use getting wound up over possibilities. He'd take things the way they came. If he couldn't do the job Troy had given him, he'd tell her and be on his way.

He grinned when he put on the new clothes he had bought. No use fooling himself. He wouldn't be on his way for a long time. Not until he'd explored that soft streak of Troy's. Remembrance of the kiss she had given him had been riding with him all day.

He finished dressing, feeling a little uncomfortable in the store suit and white shirt. The collar and black tie choked him. He had always hated a tie. Troy was asking more of him than she realized. He buckled his gun belt around his waist, picked up his worn range clothes, and left the bathroom.

The barber looked at him and shook his head. "You're wearing the wrong duds, friend."

"I reckon not." Jim paid him for the bath and shave. "How long has this Knoll hombre been riding for Pollock?"

"As long as I've been in the valley. Ten years or more. Why?"

"Just curious. Ever know a fellow named Manders?"

The barber stepped back, his long-fingered hands fluttering uncertainly. He was suddenly as wary as a forest animal that has been frightened. "Yeah, I knew him."

"I'm here to buy the Manders place. Who owns it?"

"I — I don't know." The barber's breath sawed out of him. "Look, friend. You've got

50

enough trouble without going out to hunt for more."

Jim grinned at him. "It's my guess I'm not the only man who's got trouble hereabouts. Who would I see about buying the Manders ranch?"

"I don't know, but if you're looking for a job I can help you. This town needs a marshal. A good one. I've been it, but I'm not a good one. I just resigned."

"So did I," Jim said. "Before I was hired."

He walked out, leaving the barber staring bleakly at his back. The street was still deserted, and the only horses in sight were the two racked in front of the saloon. Probably belonged to Pollock's men. It was dusk now, and Jim couldn't tell for sure about the horses. Not unless he walked across the street and had a close look, and it didn't seem important enough for that.

Jim went into the hotel and asked for a room. The clerk nodded and turned the register for Jim to sign. He gave Trinidad as his address, which was as good as any for a man who didn't have an address. Bob Jarvis's name was directly above his. Room 12. If the even-numbered rooms were on the same side of the hall, 10 and 12 would be together, with a thin wall between.

Curiosity was nagging at him again. Apparently Bob Jarvis and the girl weren't going to be allowed to leave town alive. You never knew all the angles on such a deal, but if Jim was guessing right he and Jarvis were caught in the same loop.

"How long does the dining room stay open?" Jim asked.

"Another hour yet."

Jim picked up his clothes. "Where does Matt Seery live?"

The clerk blinked owlishly, hesitating. It followed, Jim thought. Nobody in Bakeoven called his soul his own. Maybe Seery didn't like strangers. Or maybe the clerk had heard about the business in the barbershop.

"Don't you know him?" Jim asked.

"Sure, I know him." The clerk's Adam's apple bobbed experimentally, then he said: "Big, white house. Got a picket fence around it. Row of cottonwoods in front. A block south of Main Street."

Jim thought the clerk was going to add, "But don't tell Seery I told you." He didn't, but he was scared. It was there in the nervous twitching of his mouth, in the way his eyes kept skittering about. Just part of the contagion that everybody had tonight, maybe, waiting for Bob Jarvis to get shot; and nobody was going to raise a hand to help him.

"Thanks," Jim said, and climbed the stairs.

His room was next to Jarvis's as he had guessed. He went in as silently as he could, laid his range clothes on a chair, and moved to the wall between him and Room 10. The wall was thin, as it was in most cowtown hotels, but Jim could hear nothing for a moment except the low sobbing of a woman. Then someone began walking around, bootheels thudding against the floor.

Finally a man said, "You've got to stay here, Betty."

And the woman: "If they kill you, they might as well kill me. I'm going, Bob."

Silence for a time. Even the sobbing stopped. Suddenly the man shouted: "I won't take the stage. I'll wait till it's dark and I'll go after Seery. I'll kill him, Betty."

"They'll hang you," the woman said, "or Knoll and Perkins will shoot you. You shouldn't have brought me here. Why didn't you just leave me alone?"

"You know why. I love you. I couldn't leave you out there for Seery to — to . . ."

His voice faded away. Jim had heard enough. Seery was tied into it, too. It bore out what Troy had said. Seery and Pollock were together. Maybe this was as good a place to start as any.

Jim left the room and knocked on Jarvis's

door. No answer. He knocked again, calling, "Jarvis, I want to talk to you."

The door opened a crack, and Jim looked into the muzzle of a cocked Colt. The pale, twitching face above it belonged to a young fellow who was more boy than man. He was panicky, and therefore dangerous.

"What do you want?" Jarvis whispered.

A peach-fuzz mustache sprouted from the boy's upper lip. Trying to be a man, Jim thought, but he was reaching for something that the years hadn't yet given him. Jim said: "My name's Sullivan. I'd like to help you."

"Nobody in this God-damned town would help me. Go away. Let me alone."

"I can help you," Jim said.

"I never saw you before." Sweat ran down the boy's face and dripped from his chin. "Pollock probably sent you here. Get out now before I shoot you."

Jarvis's finger was tight on the trigger. Jim swung around and went down the stairs. The boy was a walking dead man if he didn't have help, and he knew it, but it was natural enough for him to be suspicious of any stranger.

Jim stepped into the hotel dining room, which was deserted at that late hour. A waitress came out of the kitchen, took his order, and went back through the swinging door. Darkness was complete now, for the last of the twilight had gone. Lamps had been lighted in the hotel, the saloon, and the stage office down the street.

When the waitress brought his meal, Jim asked, "When does the stage leave town?"

She was a middle-aged woman, a little gray, the crepe-like skin around her eyes showing the wrinkles that life carves in the faces of those who live constantly on the sharp edge of starvation. She said, "I don't know," and fled back into the kitchen.

Jim swore as he cut his steak. The waitress was like the clerk. A stranger worried them because they didn't know where he stood or what he would do or why he was here. He was so suspect that even an innocuous question frightened them.

There should be some time yet before the stage left. As Jim ate, gulping his food as fast as he could, he thought about the situation. It was the damnedest thing he had ever seen. Everyone in town knew what was shaping up, even the waitress. They'd wait for the inevitable, for a boy and perhaps a girl to be killed. Jim wondered how so many cowards had managed to gather in a town as small as Bakeoven.

A thought occurred to Jim that startled him. He remembered how the barber had looked him over when he'd first gone into the shop. The man had been heating a boiler of water for someone, maybe Bert Knoll. If that was true, the barber might have told Jim he could have a bath because he knew it would put him against Knoll. There was always a chance a gun-packing stranger might be faster on the draw than the local man the barber wanted killed. On the other hand, if Knoll turned out to be faster nothing would have been lost. The barber could have given Knoll some excuse: he hadn't known Knoll would be in town or the stranger had threatened him or anything of the sort. It was an idea to keep in mind about the barber, or, for that matter, the whole town. One thing was plain. No one wanted to buck Pollock or his crew, and helping the boy and girl who were upstairs in the hotel room would be bucking Pollock. He finished his steak, wondering if the waitress was going to bring him any dessert.

Then it broke, a full half-hour before he expected it. He heard the pistol-sharp crack of the stage driver's whip; he heard someone rush down the stairs and across the lobby.

Jim lunged toward the door. The stage was wheeling down the street, the driver yelling and pouring the silk to his horses. Jim ran across the lobby and into the street. He saw

Jarvis out there in the deep red dust, motioning to the driver and screaming, "Let me on, Bruce; let me on."

But the stage gathered speed and roared past Jarvis, who rushed after it, clawing at the back boot like a panicky animal trying to duck into his hole before a hunter's bullet reaches him. Then the guns sounded, drowning out the crack of the driver's whip, and Jarvis fell face down into the dust, hands thrown out in front of him. The stage rolled on out of town and thundered across the bridge.

Jim's .45 was in his hand. The killers were standing in front of the saloon, boldly, as if they had no fear of trouble, as if they were sure they were above all human law and judgment. Jim fired as Jarvis fell. He got a man with his first shot, sending him spilling back through the batwings of the saloon. The other ran. Bert Knoll, Jim thought, and threw a shot after him. He missed. The man, out of the patch of light, fired back. Close, too close.

Jim was caught in the light from the hotel behind him. He dropped flat, a second bullet kicking up dust inches from his left shoulder. He squeezed off two more shots and thought he missed. No way to be sure. Then Knoll was gone around the corner of the saloon.

A girl ran out of the hotel as men rushed into the street. She knelt in the dust and cradled Jarvis's head in her lap, saying over and over, "Bob, Bob." Jim rose and holstered his gun. The barber was there. The hotel clerk. The old storekeeper. The man with the white mustache who had said he was the mayor. A half dozen more Jim had not seen before. They moved toward Jarvis, slowly, warily, the thin light in the street showing their scared, pinched faces.

Jim laid his voice against them with bitter venom: "You all knew what this boy was up against. What kind of a town is this?"

They stopped, some of them backing away, still trapped by the sucking weakness of their fear. The mayor said: "You don't need to ask, friend. You've seen what this town is."

And the barber, spiteful now: "You didn't get Bert Knoll. He'll be back."

"He won't have to hunt for me," Jim said. "I meant to save the boy's life, but I didn't know the stage was leaving so soon."

"Forty minutes ahead of schedule," the mayor said. "You can see what the town's like, all right. Take my advice and get your horse and ride out of here while you can."

"Not me," Jim said. "If you see Knoll, tell

him I'll be around."

Someone called from the saloon, "Perkins is dead."

Jim walked to where Jarvis lay, the girl still holding his head in her lap. She was crying hysterically, her slender body shaken by the violence of it. Jim knelt, and taking the boy's wrist, felt for his pulse. There was none. Jim said gently: "He's gone. There's nothing you can do for him now."

She didn't hear. She couldn't. He picked her up, and as he turned toward the hotel he saw the barber standing motionless, staring at him. Jim said, "You've got two corpses, both dirty."

"I'll have another," the barber said. "A clean one, with red hair."

Jim carried the girl into the hotel and climbed the stairs. The lamp in the room she had shared with Jarvis was still lighted. He put her down on the bed and locked the door, then pulled up a chair and sat down to wait.

CHAPTER FIVE

Presently the girl stopped crying. She lay motionless, staring blankly at the ceiling. She was a little older than Bob Jarvis had been, Jim thought, probably in her early twenties. Pretty enough, and her figure was trim, taut. Blue eyes. Hair that was close to being red. But her face held sadness and disillusionment.

Jim smoked a cigarette, a little impatient now because he still wanted to see Matt Seery tonight. He wondered if the man had been on the street with the others. He rose, put out his cigarette, and brushed the street dust from his clothes. Most of it came out, but his suit was rumpled.

He wouldn't make the impression on Seery that Troy had hoped he would. Troy would probably call him a fool for buying into the business. He paced the length of the room, asking himself why he had. A quick answer came to him. His eavesdrop-

60

ping had told him one thing which seemed important. Seery was involved in Jarvis's killing. But the answer didn't satisfy him.

He brought his chair to the side of the bed, sat down, and took the girl's hand. It was very cold. She was still staring at the ceiling, and for a moment he thought she was in some sort of coma.

He said gently: "I want to talk to you. Can you hear me?"

He saw that she was conscious. Her eyes came to him as if only then aware of his presence. She was wearing a tan blouse and a black skirt, and now she reached down to tug at her skirt, which had pulled up to her knees.

"Who are you?" she asked.

"Jim Sullivan. I came to the door a while ago and wanted to help Jarvis. I could have saved his life."

"He was too scared to listen to anyone," she said. "He wouldn't even listen to me. I'm to blame for it. I killed him. I might as well have pulled the trigger."

"Tell me about it?"

"It's none of your business."

"Yes, it is. I killed Perkins."

"Why did you butt into it?"

He frowned. She was asking the same question he had asked himself a moment ago. He couldn't tell her about Troy and why he had come to Bakeoven. Even if he did, he couldn't give her a reason that would make sense. Thinking about it, he reluctantly admitted to himself that another of his faults was that of helping someone who needed help when the whole thing was not his concern at all. He had done the same thing more than once in the past, and he had come close to being killed because of it. He had thought Troy had a soft spot. Hell, he had one himself.

"I couldn't sit around and let it happen," he said finally. "I guess I've got a talent for trouble."

"In this country you don't have to have a talent for trouble," she said. "You just have it."

"What's your name?"

"Betty Erdman."

"Go ahead. Tell me about it. Why did they kill him?"

"Because he loved me. But I was wrong. I should have known." She squeezed his hand, her eyes begging for his understanding. "Do you know what it is to be so desperate for help that you'll take anything you can, even when you know you shouldn't?"

He nodded. "I know."

"Bob rode for Nate Pollock. I've been staying at the old Manders place. My folks died and left me without anything. Pollock promised me a job, but it wasn't a job he had to offer. Everyone thinks I'm his woman. I'm bad, you see. I guess you know how that is. A woman is bad or she's good, and there's no halfway place about it."

"You weren't Pollock's woman?"

"I'm Matt Seery's." She turned her head away, and he wondered how long it had been since she had smiled. "Nobody in town knows that. Nobody would believe me if I told them."

It jolted him. He leaned back and rolled another cigarette and lighted it. He'd bought into a hell of a lot more than he had realized. Troy would say he was a fool. Seery would have nothing to do with him when he heard.

"Go on," he said.

"Seery made me a lot of promises, and I guess I was in love with him. Finally I figured out he wasn't going to marry me. He's engaged to a girl here in town. I couldn't get away by myself. They never let me have a horse. Well, Bob rode for Pollock, and he got to coming over after dark when Seery wasn't around. Finally he said he'd get me out of the country."

She stopped, her hands knotted at her sides. Jim said, "Go on."

"I sneaked away from the house and hid in the willows along the creek. Bob couldn't get another horse for me without making Pollock suspicious, so I had to ride into town behind him. We couldn't go very far that way. That was why we decided to take the stage, but Pollock must have been told by someone in town that we were in the hotel. He sent Knoll and Perkins to get Bob. I didn't want him to get on the stage, but he said it was the only way. They'd kill him if he stayed. He was going to get a job somewhere else and send for me. He said I'd be safe in the hotel."

"About Seery. Why don't people know he was your man?"

"He has a ranch out there that he'd go to, then he'd come to my place after dark. I don't think anyone knew how it was except Pollock and Bob. People around here all think Seery is too good for anything like that."

Jim rose. "Stay here. I've got the room next to yours. I've got an errand to do, but I won't be gone long."

She cried out: "Don't go into the street. They'll get you for killing Perkins."

He grinned at her. "Not me. I've got more

lives than a cat. Be sure your door is locked, and don't let anyone in but me."

He left the room and waited until he heard the lock turn, then went down the stairs and into the street. The stage office was closed and dark, and now the only lights were in the hotel and saloon. No one was in sight. Even the horses that had been racked in front of the saloon were gone.

As Jim strode down the street and turned south at the corner, he wished he knew more about Bert Knoll. What Jim had said about having more lives than a cat was true, or had been in the past because he had a strong streak of caution and a rare sense of knowing when to push and when to let caution rule him.

He had learned there were two kinds of killers: ones like Moloch Dykens, who were not above shooting a man in the back, and others who played the game by the rules. There were some men Jim could place in the right classification almost as soon as he saw them, but there were others he couldn't. Knoll was one of them.

Reaching the side street, Jim turned along it and came to Seery's home. Even in the darkness he could see that it was a sprawling two-story structure, probably built to symbolize Seery's importance, just as the stone bank building did. As Jim walked up the path to the front door, he mentally pictured Matt Seery as a pious psalm singer who used Nate Pollock to hide his sins of the flesh.

Jim stepped up on the porch that ran the full width of the house and jerked the bell pull. He could hear the metallic jingle far back in the house. Nothing happened. He waited a moment, eyes on the frosted glass in the door that was framed by small, rectangular pieces of colored glass. He could not see into the hall, but there was a light, so someone must be in the house.

He yanked the bell pull again. A moment later the door swung open. A tall, white-haired woman stood there, a lamp held high in her hand.

"Good evening," the woman said, studying Jim with the cool detachment of a born aristocrat who never for a moment doubted her superiority.

Jim removed his derby. "I want to see Mr. Seery."

The woman moved forward a step, the lamp still held high. She was in her middle fifties, Jim judged. She was wearing a black silk dress that rustled as she moved, the white lace collar fitting tightly around her skinny neck. Her lips were thin and pale, pressed together to make a severe line that was nowhere relieved by the slightest hint of a smile or good humor.

"What is your business?" the woman asked.

"My business is with Mr. Seery," Jim said curtly.

"Mr. Seery is a busy man. Whatever business you have with him will wait until morning. Then you can see him in the bank."

"No, it won't wait," Jim said.

"A man concerned with legitimate business does not wear a gun," the woman said, and started to close the door.

Jim, thoroughly angry now, put a foot across the threshold so that she couldn't close the door. He said, "Tell Seery I'm here."

She flushed, the line of her mouth more severe than ever. She said in a peremptory voice: "The hour is late. Go away. You can talk to my son in the morning."

Jim grinned at her. "So you're Matt Seery's mother. I've never seen him, but I had an idea he was a grown man. Since he isn't, I'll discuss my business with you. If you approve, I'll see him."

She hesitated, then said coldly, "He's in the study, but be sure you don't keep him up late."

Jim stepped into the hall and hung his derby on a rack. As she closed the door behind him, he said, "Your apron string is dragging, Mrs. Seery."

"You're quite wrong," she said with cold hauteur. "A stranger would not understand."

She turned and led the way down the hall, the thick Brussels carpet smothering their steps. The dark paneled oak gave Jim the depressing feeling that he had stepped into a house which was without life.

Mrs. Seery stopped outside a door, tapped on it, and called, "Matthew, there is a man here to see you." She opened the door. "You may go in." The instant Jim was in the room, she closed it behind him.

Matt Seery rose from where he had been sitting at a huge mahogany desk. He stood motionless, pale blue eyes appraising Jim, who walked to the desk and held out his hand. "I'm Jim Sullivan. You never heard of me, but I've heard of you and I've ridden a long ways to see you."

Seery gave his hand a firm grip and motioned to a dark blue plush chair. Darkness was the key to this house, Jim thought, darkness and lifelessness; and in spite of what Troy had told him about Seery he could not help feeling some sympathy for him.

"Sit down, Mr. Sullivan."

Seery had been smoking a bent-stemmed meerschaum pipe that was darkened by age. He picked it up, lighted it, and then, belatedly remembering he was the host, opened a cigar box and held it out to Jim.

"Thanks." Jim took a cigar and dropped into the plush chair. "I understand your father started this town."

Seery sat down and nodded as he leaned back in his swivel chair. Jim's mental picture of him had been completely wrong. He had expected to find a big brutal man, although when he had learned that the woman who met him at the door was Seery's mother he had altered his preconceived notion. He hadn't altered it enough.

Seery was wearing a smoking jacket of some dark plaid material. He was still clad in the white shirt and black tie that he had probably worn all day at the bank. He was tall and very thin; his face was that of a man who lived indoors, the skin pallid. His forehead was inordinately high above pale brows. But the thing that startled Jim more than his looks was the air of gentleness which seemed to be so much a part of him.

"We came here when I was a boy," Seery said. "Actually, we had no right to be in the valley because the Utes had not been officially moved to their new reservation in Utah, but red tape never stopped my father. In time he received title to the town site." Seery motioned toward a gilt-framed picture on the wall. "That was my father, Alexander Seery. He was murdered twelve years ago."

"Murdered?"

Seery nodded. "One night when he was alone in the bank. We never found out who did it."

Jim swung around to look at the picture, a little stunned by the knowledge that the elder Seery had been murdered. Troy had neglected to tell him that. Jim studied the bold face with its saber-sharp nose and its sweeping mustache. Alexander Seery had been born to command, and Jim, thinking about Mrs. Seery, wondered how they had got along. Matt, who looked as if he was a scholar, didn't seem to be a son who would have fitted into the Seery way of life. Perhaps he hadn't. It might account for Mrs. Seery's attitude toward him.

"Must have been quite a man," Jim said, turning back to face Seery.

"He was." Seery smiled around the stem of his pipe. "Quite a man. He built the bank building which you have undoubtedly noticed. His idea was that you could have a strong bank in a frame building and people wouldn't trust it, but if you had a weak bank in a granite building folks would think it was going to last forever. My father understood people, Mr. Sullivan."

"He must have," Jim said, wondering why Seery wanted to talk about his father.

"He started with very little, but he made a fortune in this valley," Seery went on. "He built the house and furnished it in a manner he could not afford, but he said folks expected a banker to live like a banker. Before he died, he had a good small ranch at the upper end of the valley which I own. He operated a stage and freight line between here and Placerville which is still very profitable. It belongs to my mother, and she also owns the bank which I manage for her. She's a very strong woman, Mr. Sullivan."

Jim pulled on his cigar, not understanding why Seery was hated by Troy and why she blamed him for her father's death. Jim had never seen a more innocuous-appearing man in his life than Matt Seery. He resembled a potato sprout that had never got out of the cellar.

"I can believe that." Jim shifted his weight in the chair. "Mr. Seery, I came to see you because I heard you were the big gun on this range."

"The big gun." Seery seemed amused as

he tapped the dottle from his pipe into a hammered copper ash tray on his desk and filled it from a humidor. "That term might apply to my mother. Or Nate Pollock. But not to me."

Jim reached into his pocket for a handful of gold coins, and spread them on the desk in front of Seery. He said: "You're the man I want. What god do you worship, Mr. Seery?"

Though the mild expression on Seery's face momentarily altered, Jim could not tell what he was thinking. The composed expression was there again, like a mask that had been removed and immediately replaced.

"You're a strange person, Mr. Sullivan," Seery said, "and you ask a strange question. Well, I went to church with my mother when I was a boy, but I suppose I worship a metal god the same as you do."

Jim put the money back into his pocket. "I'm a rough man, Mr. Seery, but there are some things I understand. Making money is one of them. I represent a million dollars which is to be invested somewhere. Some of it could come to this valley, but if you're not interested, it's no go."

Seery had lighted his pipe. Now he reached down, and picking up a small Maltese kitten, put it on his lap and began stroking it. He said: "You interest me a great deal. Go on."

"I want to buy the Manders place."

Seery's eyes were on the kitten, the mask of composure remaining in place. "I'm afraid that's impossible. Manders was killed several years ago by outlaws, and his daughter still has title to the ranch. She doesn't live here, so Pollock has been using her grass, but you can't buy it from him."

The kitten began to purr. It annoyed Jim, who was not a cat lover. He said sharply: "Look, Seery. I know something about the situation. I met the Manders woman. She has a ranch in the Neutral Strip. When I talked to her, she said she intended to come back. There must be some way to encourage her to come, or at least get in touch with her."

Seery shook his head. "I don't know how we could."

"If this is the right place," Jim said, "and I've heard it is, my people will invest, but they won't dilly-dally around."

"Why do you want the Manders place?"

Jim fingered the ash from his cigar. This was the moment he had been working up to, and he knew Troy's plan would fail or succeed now. He said: "One sure way to make money is to promote an irrigation system. From what the Manders woman told me, I judge there's a sizable stream that has its source on Telescope Mountain and flows across her land. She said there was a natural reservoir site on her property."

"She's right." Seery was still looking at the cat, his high forehead furrowed in a frown. "You understand, of course, that there would be hell to pay if you started talking irrigation. Most of the valley land is not patented and would be open for settlement, but the local ranchers would fight."

"I'm not afraid of a fight," Jim snapped. "What's more, my people have means of advertising. If we put in a ditch system, I'll guarantee we'll have a thousand settlers in this valley by spring."

"Why do you need me?" Seery asked, looking up.

"To give advice. You know these people. You can tell me who can be scared and who will sell and who won't. Since I'm a stranger, it would take me a long time to learn that. A second reason is that you run the bank. We need you. You'll give the settlers credit. By the time they have proved up, they'll be in debt to the bank. You'll close them out, we'll bring in a new crop of settlers, and we'll sell the land over."

Seery stroked the cat softly. "How much would I make out of this?"

"Maybe a hundred thousand. Depends, of course; but my idea was to split fifty-fifty."

"But I'm to stay out for the time being? Work undercover, you might say?"

"That's right. We'll take the risks."

Seery put the kitten down and rose. "Tell me one thing, Mr. Sullivan. I saw you ride into town on a tired horse. You looked like a cowhand just in off the range. You come here dressed up. Why?"

Jim laughed. "I'm an engineer. I get around faster and with less trouble in the cattle country if I look like a cowhand, but I knew I wouldn't get into your house looking like a saddle bum."

"Quite right." Seery knocked his pipe out and put it down on the desk. "Let me think about this tonight. Nate Pollock is the man who will give us trouble. He's a rough man, Mr. Sullivan — a good deal rougher than you are, I think."

"I can handle him if it comes to that." Jim rose, his jaws taking a new grip on the tattered cigar stub in the corner of his mouth. "I'll drop over to the bank in the morning. I want you to show me the Manders place."

"Glad to do it." Sullivan walked to the

door and opened it. "Good night, Mr. Seery."

"Matt." A girl was running down the hall. "Matt."

Seery frowned, plainly irritated by the interruption. "Come in, Lily."

She was blond and quite young, eighteen probably, Jim judged. She was pale and panting, and so excited that she was almost hysterical. She rushed into the room, Mrs. Seery following sedately behind her. The girl cried, "Matt —"

"Lily, I want you to meet Mr. Sullivan," Seery broke in. "Sullivan, this is my fiancée, Lily Darket."

"I'm pleased to meet you," Jim said.

The girl glanced at Jim briefly. She wasn't pretty, not nearly so pretty as Betty Erdman. It was the kind of situation that enlisted Jim's curiosity at once. He glanced at her left hand. The diamond was the biggest one he had ever seen, a Seery symbol, like the granite bank building and the Seery house.

She said, "How do you do," and turned back to Seery. "Matt, did you hear the gun shots a while ago?"

"He has been in the study all evening," Mrs. Seery said. "He wouldn't be able to hear them with his windows and door closed."

"No, I didn't hear any shots," Seery said.

"Bob Jarvis was shot and killed by two of Pollock's men," the girl cried, running the words together in her haste. "Jarvis had brought the Erdman girl to town, but she didn't try to get on the stage. Then someone, a stranger, butted in and killed Perkins and wounded Knoll."

The information should have been a terrible shock to Seery if he hadn't heard, but Jim, watching him closely, could not see the slightest change of expression on his face. He asked quietly, "What are you so excited about?"

"Daddy says . . ." The girl stopped and licked her lips. "It's enough to be excited about. What will Pollock do? He hasn't had a man killed for as long as I can remember. He might — might burn the town."

"Quit worrying." Seery smiled. "Pollock isn't quite that bad. Who was this stranger?"

"Me," Jim said. "I'll see you in the morning," and pushing past the girl, he left the room.

Seery had either heard about it and therefore was prepared for the news, or he had the most complete control over his emotions of any man Jim had ever seen. There was a third possibility. The Erdman girl might have lied about her relationship with Seery, but Jim could not think of any reason why she would. And if Seery had been in the study all evening, he couldn't have heard. No, Seery must be a cold fish, the coldest Jim had ever run into.

He reached the hall rack and had his derby in his hand before he realized that Mrs. Seery had followed him. When he looked at her defiant face, he sensed that she was afraid of him and therefore hated him. She liked her life; she had no intention of altering it. Instinctively, she would be worried about any stranger, particularly a tough one like Jim Sullivan.

"You will leave town at once," she said harshly. "Do not see Matthew in the morning."

He grinned at her. "Sounds like you give the orders."

"I do," she said. "To everyone except. Nate Pollock. If you are trying to persuade Matthew to help you, you will only succeed in injuring him. Pollock is that kind of man."

"Don't worry about your son," Jim said. "I'll take care of Pollock."

He turned the gold-plated doorknob, opened the door, and left the house. A tall evening, he thought, as he walked back to the hotel, a very tall evening. He had made some enemies tonight, and only one friend, Betty Erdman, who would be of no help to him. But he had learned one interesting fact: Mrs. Seery was not so sure of the Seery position in the valley as Jim had supposed. She was desperately afraid of Nate Pollock.

He crossed the lobby and climbed the stairs, wondering what Matt Seery would think of his proposition and of him, now that he knew Jim had killed Perkins. He'd find out in the morning. Then he stopped dead still in the hall, his heart hammering. Betty Erdman's door was open. The room was empty. He went in. There was no sign she had ever been there. He swung to the door and examined it. It had been smashed open.

He stood there, swearing softly. What kind of a God-damned town was this that would let a girl be kidnaped? Seery might not have known what had happened, but he certainly had men working for him, Nate Pollock's men.

Well, Jim could do nothing tonight. Betty was probably safe enough. Tomorrow he'd have a look at the Manders house. If she was there, he'd fetch her back to the hotel. If she wasn't . . . Hell, she had to be. They wouldn't take her to Seery's house.

He went into his room, still thinking about it. The instant he stepped through the door, a powerful blow struck him on the neck and knocked him to his knees. He heard Bert Knoll say, "When I tell a son of a bitch like you to leave town, he'd better go." A boot slammed into his back and he toppled forward on his face.

CHAPTER SIX

Gabe Dykens did not look back at Jim Sullivan after they split on Starlight Mesa. He had considered forcing the issue, and decided against it. At the moment it was enough to worry Jim. Maybe he'd fail at the job Troy had given him. Troy would have no use for him if he did, and that would be the time to kill him. From the time Gabe had signed on with Troy, he had been careful not to offend her.

The piñons thinned out. Suddenly Gabe sensed that Moloch was swinging to the right. He understood the simple working of his brother's mind. Moloch knew that Gabe wanted Jim killed, and he saw no reason to wait.

Gabe said, "Let him go, Molly."

"But, hell —" Molly began.

"Let him go," Gabe said patiently. "Troy gave him a job. Plenty of time to beef him after he does it."

You needed patience with Moloch. A harsh word and he'd sulk for days. He was like a one-man dog. A little kindness went a long way. But now Enoch made the mistake of laughing at Moloch. He said, "A little anxious, ain't you, Molly?"

"Shut up, Enoch," Gabe said.

"Yeah, you shut your God-damned mug," said Moloch, taking his cue from Gabe. "Some day I'm gonna blow a hole right through your gizzard."

"Don't pay no attention to him," Gabe said. "He ain't very bright."

"Naw," Moloch said with satisfaction, "he ain't bright."

They were crossing a meadow, the grass knee-high on the horses. Enoch pulled up beside Gabe, his big face dark with anger. Gabe knew that their frail alliance was going to blow up some day and that one of his brothers would kill the other. It infuriated him that he had to keep them apart. He needed them, or he would have let them have it out a long time ago.

"Which way do you reckon we'd better head, Enoch?" Gabe asked.

Asking Enoch for advice usually worked, for he never seemed to figure out that Gabe was always one jump ahead of him and had the answer before he asked the question. It was much the same with Moloch when he told him Enoch wasn't bright. Enoch always got sore, but nothing made Moloch feel so good as being told he was mentally superior to Enoch. It was a sort of juggler's act, like keeping two balls in the air at the same time.

"I don't see much sense to hanging to this rim," Enoch said. "Chances are they'll have their cow camp somewhere in the middle of the mesa."

Gabe waited a moment so that Enoch would think he was giving the remark careful thought, then he nodded. "I guess you're right. Let's swing north a little. We'll pick up a trail maybe."

They topped a low ridge and found themselves in a scrub oak thicket. They slowed up, for they had to duck and twist and circle around to get through the oak brush. It would be hell getting old mossyhorns out of this stuff, Gabe thought.

If Seery's crew had the beef herd gathered, they'd be plenty sore about having to do the job over again. And Seery would be sore when he found out about it. They might have snow before the steers were gathered again. They'd be late shipping, then they'd have to return and round up the cows and calves. Seery would have a knot tied in his tail for sure.

Then Gabe thought about Troy. He'd never figured her out. All he knew was that he'd wanted her from the day she'd saved his and his brothers' necks. He'd never given her a hint of his feelings. He'd never even touched her. The longer he had been around her, the more unattainable she had seemed.

At times Gabe wondered if Troy had a woman's feelings. Maybe there was something wrong with her. But after last night he knew there wasn't. She'd picked her man, and the man was Jim Sullivan. Now, thinking about the hour or more they had spent alone at the riverbank, Gabe let his hatred for Jim grow until it became a poison in him. He wished he'd let Moloch shoot Jim in the back. Troy would have blamed it on one of Seery's riders.

"Here's your trail," Enoch said.

Gabe had been so deep in his thoughts that he hadn't been seeing anything. He reined up, cursing himself. A man was a fool to let a woman get such a hold of him. As soon as this business was finished, he'd tell Troy how he felt. If Jim was out of the way, she'd turn to him. She'd better, he thought as he dismounted, if she knew what was good for her. There were plenty of other women in the world, women who knew they were women.

He knelt beside the trail that at this point ran directly north and south. Three horses had passed, headed south, probably early this morning. It was a good guess they'd left the cow camp to comb the brush along the rim. Gabe rose and glanced up at the sun. The afternoon was half gone. Seery's crew would be back at the cow camp before dark with the steers they'd found. They wouldn't tackle driving a bunch of spooky critters through the brush after dark.

He stepped back into the saddle and motioned Enoch to the north. "I figure the cow camp's that way."

He took the lead now, warily. He didn't want to run into Seery's riders. There probably was no danger. Still, strangers would naturally be suspected, and Gabe was remembering Troy's orders not to get the law on their tails. The job had to be done from a distance, and with a certain amount of caution.

They rode steadily for two hours, the trail twisting to the northwest through low scattered brush. There were an occasional cedar and a good deal of yucca and cactus. The grass was good, and it struck Gabe that if Seery had this mesa to himself he was a fool for not putting twice the number of cattle up here that he did. Apparently Seery did have it to himself, for they saw a number of cows and calves, all carrying the Horseshoe Bar iron.

The sun was dropping fast, and Gabe was beginning to doubt his judgment when they topped a low rise and saw the cow camp directly ahead in a clearing. Gabe reined up, motioning for Enoch and Moloch to stop. For a moment he sat studying the layout. Just a cabin and pole corral, with a barbed-wire fence to the west around a stretch of meadow. Gabe judged that about ninety head of steers were held inside the fence.

"No cover here," Enoch said. "We'd better get into them piñons yonder."

Gabe nodded, mentally debating if it would be better to duck back over the ridge and wait until dark. It would be a simple matter to work up close to the cabin, get the drop on Seery's men, and start them walking toward town. Then they'd burn the cabin, let the horses out of the corral, and run the steers back into the brush.

He was still turning it over in his mind when Enoch said: "They're coming, three of 'em. Looks like they've got eight, ten critters with 'em."

They were angling in from the south,

riding wearily. Damned fools, Gabe thought as he swung his horse and rode back down the ridge, wearing themselves out digging old mossyhorns out of the scrub oak for a banker who kept his seat warm in town while these boys made money for him.

He laughed silently when he thought about their long walk to town, and what Matt Seery would say when they showed up and told him what had happened. Too bad Gabe couldn't tell these boys that this was Troy Manders's doing.

"Well?" Enoch asked.

"Let's bust 'em," Moloch said. "The light's good enough for shooting."

"No," Gabe said. "We'll circle around to them piñons."

It took several minutes to reach the piñons, a black wall that gave adequate cover and was close enough to the camp for Gabe to watch the crew's movements. He said, "We'll wait here till it gets dark." He dismounted and stretched, feeling the need for a cigarette and knowing he couldn't have one.

Enoch stood beside him, peering through the piñon limbs. "Them boys are tired," he said. "Brush popping in that damned scrub oak ain't to my liking. Wonder what kind of summer graze Troy has?"

"What we can take for her, I reckon."

Enoch scratched his fat nose and turned to Gabe. "You ain't said much lately. I've been wondering."

The three cowhands had turned their day's gather into the pasture and had ridden to the corral. Gabe watched them. One was an old-timer, stooped and whiskery. The others were young, hardly more than boys. Gabe asked absently, "Wondering what?"

"About staying. Hell, we've stuck with Troy for two years. I've got an itch in my feet lately. We never stayed on a job for two years before. Sure, you're sweet on Troy, and that's your business, but me, I figger we've paid her what we owe her for saving our necks, and then some."

Gabe gave him a sharp look. Enoch was usually pliable enough, and he hadn't given Gabe any trouble for a long time. Now there was a stubborn set to his rough-featured face. Gabe said sharply, "We ain't pulling out when Troy's biting off a chunk of trouble like she is now."

Enoch laughed jeeringly. "So you're gonna be neighborly when Jim Sullivan's getting —"

"Shut up," Gabe breathed. "Shut up or I'll forget you're my —"

Gabe, distracted by Enoch, had forgotten to watch Moloch. Now he heard the rifle shots to his right and a little behind him, three of them, running out together so fast that the second and third hammered into the echo of the first. It was over before Gabe could stop Moloch.

Seery's men had started toward the cabin from the corral. They had been strung out, the old one in front, and they had gone down like three upended dominos when the first is tipped over. Gabe grabbed the Winchester from Moloch, yelling, "You know better'n . . ." He stopped. Patience, he told himself. Damn it, he had to have patience.

Moloch, the brown tip of his tongue lodged in the gap of his teeth, gave Gabe a hurt look. "I got 'em, didn't I?" he whimpered. "I made it easy, didn't I?"

"Yeah, sure, you made it easy." Gabe handed the Winchester back to him. "Yeah, you sure did."

"Easy, you say?" Enoch shouted. "Why, you God-damned bastard, you made it easy to put a rope on our necks, that's what you done."

Moloch whipped his rifle up and eared back the hammer. "You ain't gonna cuss

me no more. I'm gonna blow your gizzard
—"

Gabe batted the rifle barrel down. "Ease up, Molly. You've got to allow for Enoch. You know that."

Molly eared down the hammer of his rifle. "Yeah, I savvy." He cackled, the tip of his tongue working back and forth in the gap of his teeth. "He ain't bright, Enoch ain't, but me, I done a good job just now."

Gabe swung to his horse and mounted. Enoch was right. Moloch would get a rope around their necks, some other time if not today. But what could he do? He had to look out for Moloch. There were few ties of loyalty that bound Gabe, but his feeling for his brother was one. It had started a long time ago, when the three of them had run away from home. Funny. He had never really figured out the why of it. Moloch needed him. He was so damned helpless at times. And useful.

But now Gabe's sense of caution, which constantly dictated his behavior, brought a sense of panic rushing through him. More than once Moloch had got him and Enoch into trouble. That's the way it had been the time Troy had saved their lives. They'd found the wrecked stage and the wounded driver lying beside the treasure box that had been broken open. Moloch had killed the driver before Gabe could stop him.

"I done him a favor," Moloch had said defensively, as if he knew he'd done something he shouldn't. "He ain't hurting nowhere now."

But the sheriff never got the straight of it. Gabe had ordered Moloch to keep his mouth shut, and he had. The posse took them to town. Apparently no one had held the slightest doubt about their guilt. Gabe could still feel the rope around his neck before Troy and her boys had rescued them. It was the only time in his life that Gabe had been really scared, and he wouldn't forget it as long as he lived.

Gabe mounted and rode out of the pines. He didn't care much now what happened to either Enoch or Moloch. They could kill each other for all he cared. Enoch had turned sullen, and Moloch wasn't to be trusted. Gabe told himself he'd be better off without either one of them.

No use reminding Moloch what Troy's orders had been. He'd forgotten. Maybe he couldn't remember anything for more than a few hours. Or maybe he'd just acted on impulse. Anyhow, Gabe knew he should have been watching him, and he knew, too, that Troy would blame him.

He dismounted beside the three dead men. All of them had been hit dead center on a line between their noses and their belt buckles. One thing could be said for Moloch. He could shoot a fly off a man's nose as far as he could see the fly and not touch the man, only he wouldn't. He was never one to shoot a fly if he could get a man in his sights. The hell of it was, he was getting worse all the time, the way whisky or the gambling fever gets hold of some men.

Moloch and Enoch had ridden up and stepped down. "Light's a little thin," Moloch said with childlike pride. "I done pretty good."

Gabe didn't look at Enoch. He knew what was coming. Enoch would pull out the first chance he had. Gabe said, "We'll drag 'em inside."

Nevertheless he didn't move for a moment. He seldom felt any sympathy for a dead man, but he couldn't help it now as he stared at the old one's face, with the withered skin pulled tightly over his cheekbones and liver-brown lips parted from scraggly teeth. No reason for them to die. He had nothing against them. Neither did Moloch.

Shrugging, Gabe lifted the old man and

carried him into the cabin. He went through the dead man's pockets, hunting for money. Enoch brought another body in, dumped it down, and walked out. He didn't say a word. He didn't need to. One look at his stormy face told Gabe what Enoch was thinking.

Moloch came in with the third body. He dropped it, saying, "Damn it, I got him a little high." He kicked the dead man in the ribs. "Must have been the light."

Gabe searched them as he had the old man, taking only money, then he rummaged in a corner that held the grub, found a flour sack, and filled it with biscuits and bacon and some cans of tomatoes. Enoch was waiting outside. He'd have ridden off, Gabe thought, if he hadn't been afraid Moloch would shoot him.

"I done a good job, didn't I?" Moloch asked. "You're gonna tell Troy, ain't you?"

"No." Gabe laid a hand on Moloch's arm. "We won't tell anybody. A lot of folks are like Enoch. They wouldn't savvy about this."

"But Troy, she'd like to know . . ."

"No. She might tell somebody."

Moloch frowned, torn between his long-established habit of obeying Gabe and his desire to please Troy. Finally he said, "Yeah, she might tell somebody."

Gabe picked up a lamp from the table and threw it against the wall. It broke, the kerosene running across the floor. Gabe lighted a match and dropped it into the kerosene, and when he was sure the cabin would burn he jerked his head at Moloch and went outside.

Enoch had opened the corral gate and chased the horses through it. Moloch was tightening his cinch when Gabe rode up to Enoch. Gabe said: "We'll turn them steers out and get moving. Got to hole up for a day or two until we know Troy's in the valley."

"He's an idiot," Enoch breathed. "Just a God-damned backshooting idiot. You gonna plug him, or you want me to?"

Gabe pulled an ear. Funny, he thought, the way things went. Enoch was right. But shooting Moloch would be like shooting a pet hound. Even if the hound got into somebody's chicken pen, he couldn't pull the trigger on him. That had happened once when he'd been a kid. He'd loved the hound. Maybe he loved Moloch. He didn't really know.

"I can't," Gabe said. "You ain't gonna do it, neither." He wheeled his horse toward the pasture gate, calling, "Let's get these steers to moving, Molly."

For the first time in his life Gabe felt absolutely helpless. Troy was bound to find out. She wouldn't stand for disobedience, and she wouldn't stand for murder. Even if he told her how it had happened, she would blame him.

Then the awful truth began gnawing at him. He would never have her, not of her free will. Then he swore. It didn't make much difference. She was going to need him, especially after Jim Sullivan was rubbed out. He'd take her the first time he was alone with her, and then she'd belong to him. She was too proud to tell anyone. It was that simple, once Sullivan was out of the way. Hell, he might even marry her.

CHAPTER SEVEN

A smaller, softer-muscled man than Jim would have had his neck broken by that first down-swinging blow. As it was, he was momentarily paralyzed. He lay on his belly, face against the floor, pain flashing along his spine where he had been kicked.

A man lighted the lamp on the bureau. He said, "Here's one tough drifter who's gonna wish he'd never seen Rampart Valley."

Bert Knoll said, "He's gonna wish he hadn't plugged Perkins and busted my arm, too." He kicked Jim in the side. "On your feet, redhead. I've still got one good hand, and I'm gonna use it to push that ugly nose of your'n a little more to one side of your face."

"Hold on, Bert," the first man said. "He's out cold. I aim to make him talk before we finish him. He's got some kind of a slick scheme up his sleeve or he wouldn't have raised so much hell."

"Might be a U.S. marshal, Nate," Knoll said. "Go through his clothes. If he's got a badge, we'd better tote him out of here. Wouldn't do to have 'em find his carcass."

Jim had no idea how many men were in the room or whether any of them had a gun on him. But his mind cleared while he lay there. He braced his hands against the floor, knowing he could move. He had to, or be murdered. There was no doubt about their intentions.

"Go through his clothes," the man called Nate said. "Pull his iron, too, Ace."

"Hell, he plugged Perkins," a third man said. "Let's get it over with."

"Do what you're told," the other snapped. "He can't talk if he's dead, and I want to hear him talk."

Ace grumbled, but he knelt beside Jim, a hand gripping his shoulder to turn him over. In that instant Jim came alive. He rose to his hands and knees, his head snapping back so that the top of his skull caught Ace on the chin, his teeth cracking together with a staccato click.

It took a second for Jim to come up to his feet and wheel, right hand sweeping his gun from leather. He heard Knoll's shouted warning, heard the man called Nate curse.

He glimpsed Knoll standing by the door, and he saw the other one, a black-jowled, grossly fat man, and that was all. The roof fell on him, and he went down again, out cold this time.

Jim was lying on the bed when he came to. Several minutes passed before he remembered what had happened, several minutes of slow mental groping. Red flashes appeared before his eyes, and his head hurt with a throbbing ache that threatened to blow the top of his skull off. When what had happened came back to him, he was surprised to find that he was still alive.

Jim tried to sit up, but he dropped back at once. The slight movement increased the hammering in his head so that for a moment he thought he was going to faint. A man said: "Just lie there, friend. You won't get hurt any more for a while. What happens tomorrow or the day after tomorrow is another proposition."

The voice was vaguely familiar, but a headache like his did not encourage a man's memory. He managed to twist around, teeth clenched against the tide of agony that swept through him, until he saw a man with a white mustache sitting in the cane-bottom chair, his feet on the edge of the bed. He was smoking a corncob pipe, placid and apparently very comfortable, the chair tilted back, the front legs a good six inches off the floor. Then Jim remembered. It was the mayor.

"It'll take a while to get your sense back," the man said in a friendly tone. "Maybe it'll take longer for you to feel like talking, but if you feel like listening I'll do the talking for a while."

"Sure." Jim's voice sounded unfamiliar to his own ears, perhaps because of the constant throbbing pain that screwed everything out of focus. "I can listen."

"I saved your life," the man said around the stem of his pipe. "That puts you in my debt, and I like to collect when a man owes me something. However, I have an idea my notion of how you'll repay that debt will fit into what you want to do anyhow. Pollock was here with Knoll and another one of his boys named Ace Rush. I persuaded them to leave, which wasn't hard since I had a gun on them, so you'll live to fight another day."

The man eased the front legs of his chair back to the floor, and reaching under the bed, pulled out the slop jar, knocked the dottle from his pipe into it, and shoved it back. "My name's Jess Darket. I own the livery stable and a small ranch on the river.

I'm also the mayor, which is a questionable honor since no one else wanted the job."

Darket pulled a sack of tobacco from his pocket and filled his pipe. He tamped it down, reached for a match, and lighted it. He was an average-sized, mild-appearing man, perhaps fifty, endowed with a dignity and quiet strength that aroused Jim's respect. The name seemed familiar. Jess Darket. Then he remembered. Seery's girl was Lily Darket.

"You're going to be Matt Seery's father-in-law," Jim said.

Darket tipped his chair back, the lines of his face touched by surprise. "How did you know?"

"I came to Bakeoven to see Seery," Jim said. "I was with him last night when your daughter came in. She *is* your daughter, isn't she?"

Darket nodded, eyeing Jim as he pulled on his pipe, clouds of smoke drifting toward the ceiling. "So you came here to see Matt."

He did not state it as a question, but it was meant to be one. Jim said, "I'm hoping to interest him in an investment."

"I see," Darket said, as if he didn't see at all. "Well, Sullivan, you arouse my curiosity. I've followed every move you've made since you rode into Bakeoven except the visit you made to Matt. I was in the harness room in the stable when you left your horse. I watched you go to the store and come out with new duds. I watched you go into the barbershop and I know how you stood up to Bert Knoll. I know you jumped into the shooting with both feet. Now just what sort of an investment are you trying to interest Matt in?"

Jim hesitated, wondering how much he could tell this man, and decided to tell him nothing because he was the father of the girl Matt Seery was going to marry. "I just couldn't sit around and let the kid get killed. What happened to the girl?"

Darket shrugged. "I suppose they took her back to the Manders place where she's been living. Pollock wouldn't let her get away. You probably didn't know, being a stranger, but she's Pollock's woman. Apparently she just got tired of him. She wasn't worth your trouble, Sullivan."

"She's Seery's woman, not Pollock's," Jim said.

Darket jumped up and grabbed the pipe out of his mouth. "Where'n hell did you hear that?"

"She told me."

"Oh." Darket sat down and put his pipe into his mouth again. "Well, she's lying, although I see no reason for it. If you weren't a stranger, you'd know. Matt Seery isn't that kind of a man. I couldn't ask for a better husband for my girl." He laughed shortly. "You startled me for a moment."

That, Jim thought, was an understatement. Now he understood how Darket had been able to persuade Pollock and his men to leave. As Seery's future father-in-law, he carried a great deal of weight, more weight than a gun could give him.

"Well, I can't sit here all night talking, so I'll come to the point." Darket took the pipe out of his mouth and stared at it. "In the years I've been here, we've never had a man hit town and shake it up as you have. You see, we're so far from the county seat that we have practically no law. We're close to the Utah line, and for that reason our valley is a thoroughfare for outlaws who want to get out of the state fast, or hide out on Telescope Mountain."

"Pollock and Knoll were worried about me being a U.S. marshal," Jim said. "Why?"

"I figured you were," Darket said. "I've had an idea for a long time that Pollock has a profitable sideline protecting outlaws from the law, but it's just a theory. Might be good enough to interest a U.S. marshal, though."

"I'm not."

"Well now, I wish you were." Darket tapped his pipe against the palm of his hand. "So you're here to interest Matt in an investment." He shook his head. "It won't do, friend. It just doesn't account for all the antics you've been up to."

"All right," Jim said wearily. "It won't do."

Darket pulled on his pipe, but finding it cold, struck a match and lighted it again. "Well, I'm not a man to inquire into your reason. I had one purpose in coming here tonight and only one, but I did save your life." He leaned forward, gray eyes pinned on Jim's face. "I want you to repay me by taking the marshal's star. We can't touch Pollock until we can get a deputy permanently located here, but we must control what goes on in town. You showed last night you can do that."

"I'm sorry," Jim said. "I have other fish to fry."

Darket rose and jammed the pipe into the pocket of his corduroy coat. "Is that your final answer?"

"It's final," Jim answered. "As for saving my life, thanks."

"That's easy, friend, too easy." Darket studied Jim, not willing to give up. "I pride myself on being something of a philosopher, Sullivan. I would put it this way. A man who faces the sun always has his shadow falling behind him."

"Not being a philosopher," Jim said, "I don't savvy."

"Why, the figure of speech is simple enough. It's my guess you're on the dodge. If you want to hide out in our town, and if you want to make us so grateful that you will always be safe here, you'll take the star. We ask only one thing. See that Nate Pollock and his crew stay in line."

"I'm sorry," Jim said. "My fish need frying. I'd be handicapped wearing a star."

"I see." Darket moved to the door and opened it. "If you change your mind, look me up."

Darket went out, pulling the door shut. Jim sat up, and when the waves of dizziness tapered off he rose and poured water from the gaudily painted pitcher into the washbowl. His body was one great throbbing ache: his head, the base of his neck, his back, his ribs. He poured the water into the slop jar, propped the chair against the door, blew out the lamp, and lay down.

He wondered what Troy would say to him. He'd got his tail in a crack and put a good squeeze on it. Maybe taking the star wouldn't be such a bad idea. At least it would give him a legitimate reason for staying in Bakeoven.

He had to see Troy before she reached town. She should be calling the turn. She had been right about one thing even if she had been gone for nine years. These people thought Matt Seery could do no wrong.

He finally fell asleep, stirring often, and waking at every noise he heard in the hall, hand automatically reaching for the gun he had slipped under his pillow. Boogery, he told himself, so damned boogery he'd probably shoot a drunk if he stumbled into the room. Near dawn, he slept soundly.

CHAPTER EIGHT

Matt Seery turned his back to Lily Darket the instant Jim left the study. He walked to the desk and filled his pipe, taking his time. The news Lily had brought jarred him as nothing had jarred him as long as he could remember.

Because Bob Jarvis must have been in love with Betty Erdman, or he wouldn't have tried what he had, Seery was glad the boy was dead. He didn't give a damn about Perkins or Knoll, but he cared about Betty more than he cared about anyone else except himself. The fact that she had tried to run away hit him like a blow in the belly.

"Who was that man?" Lily asked. "And why did he jump into Jarvis's trouble?"

Seery didn't answer. He kept tamping tobacco into the bowl of his pipe, afraid to turn, afraid she would see something in his face that would tell her how he felt. He had several talents in which he took great pride.

One was his ability to keep anyone, particularly his mother, from knowing what his feelings were; but he knew that for a moment at least his face was an open book.

He drew a match from the pocket of his smoking jacket, deciding that Lily wasn't smart enough to detect his feelings, even now. He sat down in his swivel chair and lighted his pipe, eyes on the girl. She wasn't pretty. Her teeth were uneven, her face was freckled and often pimply, and her hair was ash blond with no life in it.

Now, staring at her, he realized how much he hated her, though she had never suspected it. He liked Betty's hair, so full of color, almost red at times, in the sunlight. As for a figure, hell, Lily was just plain dumpy. She simply had none of the trim vibrancy that he liked in Betty.

"I told you his name was Sullivan," Seery said finally, "and I have no idea why he jumped into Jarvis's fight."

He heard his mother come into the room, but he didn't look at her. His pipe had gone out, and he fumbled for another match. His mother would know something was wrong. She could always tell, and then he had to spar with her for an hour at a time until she gave up or he convinced her he was worrying about one of their businesses.

"What did the man want?" Mrs. Seery demanded.

"He had heard about the Manders place and wanted to buy it."

"Well, I'm glad he can't," Mrs. Seery said with satisfaction. "He's not the kind we want in the valley. Nate Pollock is enough."

"More than enough," Lily echoed.

She edged toward the door, looking at Seery expectantly. He rose. She wanted him to walk home with her, and he might as well do it and get rid of her. Now his mother had sensed he was upset, and she moved past Lily to the desk.

"Something's bothering you, Matthew," she said in the solicitous tone that made him furious because she was forever treating him like a child. He would never be a man in her eyes if he lived to be ninety. "If that fellow said something . . ."

"It isn't that," he said impatiently. "It was a shock to hear that young Jarvis had been shot."

He walked past his mother and took Lily's hand. She gave him her eager smile, and glancing at Mrs. Seery, said, "I'll be over in the morning, Mother."

"That will be fine," Mrs. Seery said absently, her eyes on her son's back.

Seery walked down the hall and left the

house with Lily clinging to his arm. His mother liked her because she could be managed, and he had been worn down until he proposed to her. She'd said Yes before he was finished with the proposal. She'd been in love with him ever since she'd worn pigtails, she said, but Seery had the notion she was in love with his name and money and position in the community.

Outside, on the boardwalk, Seery thought bleakly that of all the mistakes he had ever made proposing to Lily was the worst. He'd kept putting off the wedding, but sooner or later he'd run out of excuses. He'd break the engagement if he could, but she never gave him the slightest excuse. Anyhow, it would just mean another row with his mother. Some day he'd get out of the valley. He wasn't sure why he had stayed as long as he had.

Lily didn't say anything until they reached her house. He stopped at her gate, but she tugged at his arm, whispering: "Come in, Matt. Daddy's downtown somewhere. He won't be back for hours."

"I can't," he mumbled. "I've got work to do."

He simply couldn't stand her tonight. She'd want him to sit on the couch with her and kiss her. He had never gone any further than that because he might have to marry her, although she'd hinted more than once that anything was all right, now that they were engaged. But when a man had known Betty Erdman, anything Lily had to offer was like trying to do with a drink of warm, flat beer when he wanted whisky.

"Matt." She looked into his face, breathing hard. "Matt, I love you so. I can't keep on waiting. I want to get married and have our own home and start our family. Is anything keeping us from getting married?"

"Things will slack off now that it's fall," he said. "The boys will be bringing my beef herd down from the mesa in a day or two and we'll be shipping. We'll talk about a wedding date after that."

He put his pipe into his pocket. He kissed her, indifferent to the hot, feverish touch of her lips. He turned away, leaving her standing there staring after him, aware that something was wrong but not knowing what. She'd go in and lie on the couch and have a good cry, he told himself.

When he got back to the study, he found his mother waiting up for him. He said brusquely, "I've got some work to do."

"I won't stay more than a minute." Mrs. Seery clasped her long-fingered bony hands on her lap. "Matthew, you'd feel more settled if you got married. Why are you waiting?"

He sat down and laid his pipe on the desk. This was an old argument between them, part of her constant fight to dominate him and his fight to live his own life. She was a strong-willed woman who had run away from home with Alexander Seery when he had nothing except his virile good looks, a strong body, a team, and a wagon. Her husband had brought her here against her wishes when the valley was wild and un-settled. They had taken their wagon apart and let it down with ropes over the cliffs on Telescope Mountain. Seery remembered the first hard years of poverty, and he remem-bered the bitter quarrels between his father and mother, each trying to break the other's will and neither succeeding.

Seery picked up the Maltese kitten and began petting it, finding satisfaction in its contented purr. Like his horse, it was a liv-ing thing that loved him and did not try to control him. Now he could not be sure of Betty's love. He thought of how his father had died, shot by his own gun. An accident, everyone said, but Seery knew his father too well to believe that. His father had understood guns just as he had understood people, with the exception of his wife and son.

The suspicion had long been in Seery's mind that his mother had murdered his father, but he had always been afraid to mention it. Suddenly he glanced up, his eyes on his mother's arrogant face, bitter now because he had withdrawn from her. He wished she was dead. If it hadn't been for her, he would have married Betty years ago.

He wanted to sell out and leave Rampart Valley, but his mother wouldn't hear of it. She had felt as much happiness as she was capable of feeling since her husband had died. She dominated the valley in much the same way that she dominated her son; she was considered an upright and righteous woman. She was a pillar of the church, the ladies' aid, the choir, and all the other activities that stemmed from the church. That was why she wouldn't leave. It was a strange thing, because as long as her husband was alive she hated everything about the valley.

"I suppose I can't go on putting it off," he said at last. "I just hate to be tied down to a wife."

Her hands began moving nervously on her lap. Seery knew that there was something she wanted to say and that she was hesitant to say it. He had been harder for her to manage the last year or two, and he would have been even more difficult if he hadn't been afraid she'd tell him to move out to the ranch and let Vance Frane run the bank. Frane had been the cashier for years, an obnoxious tattler who ran to his mother every time Seery did something that didn't meet with Frane's approval.

"I want you to be happy, Matthew," Mrs. Seery said after a long pause. "A man needs a wife, and Lily will be a good one for you." She rose and walked to the door. For a moment she paused there, a hand gripping the gold-plated doorknob, then she said: "I want you to go to the county seat and talk to the sheriff again about sending a deputy out here. The killing tonight shows how much we need one."

That was another issue between them. Because the situation was perfect for Nate Pollock as it stood now, Seery had slyly used his influence to keep the sheriff from sending a deputy to Rampart Valley. It had been a delicate operation, skillfully done. The valley people resented having a deputy among them, Seery had said. They were law-abiding, and they felt that a town marshal in Bakeoven was all the lawman they needed. The sheriff, happy to save taxpayers' money, and knowing that no one in the county cared about the outlaws who made their escape through Rampart Valley as long as they didn't bother the local ranchers, agreed with Seery.

But tonight Seery didn't feel like arguing. He said, "I'll see about it after we ship."

She left then, saying, "Don't stay up late, Matthew."

He put the kitten down and rose. She couldn't even let him go to bed when he wanted to. He paced around the room, glancing often at his father's picture on the wall. Some day he'd yank it down and jump on it. He had hated his father, and yet, conversely, he had taken pride in his father's accomplishments.

As he had grown older, he had gradually realized that his mother was to blame for the bad feeling that had existed between him and his father. She had spoiled him. She had constantly shielded him, and insisted that he go away to school. When he was home, he must not fight. Not with the scum that lived in the valley.

His father had been furious. He had raged: "I've got a Goddamned yellow belly for a son. Ain't got a single gut in his body."

His mother had slapped his father, who had lost his temper and hit her with his fist and knocked her down. Not long after that he had been shot, and Seery was as sure as he could be sure of anything he couldn't prove that his father had brought about his own death when he had struck his wife.

Seery was not even sure why he left the picture of his father on the wall, unless it was in the hope that some day he would prove to be as tough as his father had been. Then he could stand there and laugh at it.

He loaded his pipe and pulled hard on it, filling the small room with tobacco smoke. Tonight it was not the searing memory of his father's contempt or the knowledge of his mother's dominance that caused his unrest.

He kept thinking of Betty, and of her attempt to run off with Bob Jarvis. He couldn't understand it. He had done so much for her. He had always thought she loved him. It was something he had taken for granted. Now Nate Pollock would give him the horse laugh. Probably be sore about it to boot.

Pollock would say: "I always knew that little bitch wasn't any good. She's made a fool of you, and the hell of it is folks will think it's me she's made a fool of."

But he could handle Pollock as long as he could keep Vance Frane from stealing his bank job. Pollock was up to his ears in debt to the bank. Gambling was his one great weakness. Every fall, after the beef was shipped, Pollock took a trip to one of the mining camps, usually Telluride, sat in on a poker game that would last through a couple of nights and a day, and came back broke. Then the bank would lend him more money, and he'd sink a little deeper into the pit he was digging for himself.

Seery sat down at his desk, his mind turning to Jim Sullivan. The idea of building a reservoir on the Manders property was an old one. Manders himself had pushed it before he'd been killed. It was sound enough, although the bank could not be used to promote it as long as his mother was alive. Still, there might be some way to figure a profit, and if Seery was in the driver's seat he could work it so Pollock wouldn't spoil Sullivan's game. But he'd better have a talk with Pollock before he saw Sullivan again.

Acting on impulse, he wrote a note to his mother that he had gone to the ranch. His mother would let Vance Frane know. He filled a sack with tobacco and dropped it and his pipe into a shirt pocket. He picked up the kitten, and blowing out the lamp, stepped into the hall.

He heard nothing. His mother must have

116

gone to bed. He paced along the hall to his room, lighted a lamp, and put the kitten into the box that was its bed. Seery changed to his riding clothes, buckled a gun belt around him, and slipped out through a window. As he crossed to the barn, he cursed his fear of his mother which made him sneak from the house. She'd give him hell because she thought he should spend every day in the bank.

He closed the barn door before he lit the lantern. His chestnut gelding whinnied a greeting. Seery stepped into the stall and patted the horse's neck. The gelding turned his head and nuzzled Seery, who found himself wishing that all the people in the world except Betty were animals.

He saddled the horse and backed him out of the stall. He blew out the lantern, led the horse into the alley, and closed the barn door. He rode slowly until he was out of town, not wanting to attract any attention. The cliff south of the valley was a high black wall, its rim an even line against the lighter darkness of the sky.

Courage ran in queer streaks, he thought, as he brought his chestnut into a gallop. He had climbed that wall clear to the slick rock rim, his life dependent on a thin ledge of jutting rock or shallow-rooted cedars. Not once had he been frightened. It was one thing he had done that he was proud of, one thing which even his father had been afraid to do.

He thought of other things he had done which would make most men ashamed. Like the murder of old man Manders. His father had been ruthless, but he wouldn't have done that. Seery had enjoyed it, and after all these years he could look back upon that night with pleasure.

Pollock had been willing enough because he wanted the Manders grass. He had not liked having a close neighbor like Manders, anyhow, but Seery had been prompted by quite another motive. He had run into Troy in the aspens above the Manders ranch and he had tried to kiss her. Her response had been a hard blow that bloodied his nose. It was then that he had thought of striking at her father.

His life in the valley was like walking a tight rope across a deep canyon. It was always exciting, and except for the sensual pleasure Betty gave him, his greatest satisfaction came from making people think he was an upright man when he was as crooked as a corkscrew.

He had ridden with Pollock's boys when they had rustled small bunches of valley cattle and pushed them back into the rough country of Telescope Mountain where the brands could be worked over and the cattle hidden until they healed. He had even guided outlaws into Utah with Bert Knoll, and the outlaws had never guessed he was the ultra-respectable banker from Bakeoven.

The satisfaction Betty gave him was based on much the same thing. No one knew she was his woman. Pollock was coyote-cute when it came to anything like that. If Betty told the truth, no one would believe her — not of Matt Seery, who was an upright man, a very upright man.

He reached the lane that led to Pollock's ranch, still riding fast. It lay fifty yards to his left, a group of low log buildings lost in the shadows of the huge cottonwoods that stood between them and the road. He'd see Pollock in the morning.

Half a mile farther on he passed Manders' house and saw a light in the window. For a moment he was too startled to think clearly, then he understood. Someone, probably Bert Knoll, had brought her back from town after Jarvis had been killed.

He rode on to his own place, his heart hammering. Hell, he hadn't lost her. He'd bring her around. She couldn't have been in love with a runny-nosed kid like Bob Jarvis who couldn't give her anything.

He stripped gear from his chestnut and put him into the corral because he couldn't leave him at Manders' place for anyone to see who happened to ride past. He continued to think that whatever was wrong could be fixed between him and Betty. They'd take another trip to Denver, and he'd buy her things she liked. It took a little trickery, but they had done it twice in the past. He went on business and stayed in a hotel. She came later. No one had ever found out. It was part of the pattern of being a different kind of man than anyone in the valley except Pollock and his men thought he was, a successful bit of dissembling that tickled his vanity.

He was panting when he reached the Manders house. He stopped outside until his breathing was even, for he did not want her to know he had run. Whatever happened, he must not let her know how completely she possessed him.

He crossed the porch and went in, closing the door behind him. He called, "Betty."

The door into the kitchen was open. He saw her then, bending over the range as she looked at something in the oven. For some strange reason she always started cooking when she was upset or worried. He had never understood why she did it nor how it could possibly comfort her.

She must have heard him, but she didn't look around. He strode into the kitchen, angry because she was able to ignore him. He said, "Betty, why did you run away?" The question broke out of him. He hadn't intended to ask it, and he was sorry at once that he had.

She made a slow turn to face him, the lamplight turning her hair to the reddish-gold tint he liked. It was so full of color, so alive. She was wearing a blue-flowered gingham dress that was cut to exaggerate the perfect curves of hips and breasts. He had always liked the dress, and she knew it, but he didn't think she had put it on for him tonight.

"Don't touch me, Matt," she said. "Don't ever touch me again."

He stood there, shocked by the virulence in her voice. A dark bruise showed on one side of her face where someone had struck her, probably when she had been taken from the hotel. He moved forward to the table and put his hands against it.

"Don't say that," he whispered. "You're all I've got. I love you. You know that, Betty. You've always known that."

"Love!" She threw the word at him as if it were an oath. "You don't love anyone but yourself. If you loved me, you'd have married me a long time ago. You'd walk down Bakeoven's Main Street with me instead of pretending you didn't know me when I went to town. The great Matt Seery is too good to be seen with me. You've made a damned whore out of me, and now you've got the gall to stand there and tell me you love me."

His grip tightened on the corners of the table. For the first time in his life he realized he had not been as clever as he had thought, for his very cleverness had deprived him of the one thing he wanted most of all, the thing he had taken for granted.

"You aren't being fair," he cried. "We've had good times together. Here and in Denver. You've had all you could expect."

"Fair!" She laughed at him. "That's a funny word for you to use." Then her face was gray, the laughter gone from her. "Tonight you killed Bob Jarvis. Or I did, because I was using him to get away from you."

Suddenly he was angry at what he believed was the injustice of her attitude. He had been kind to her. He had honestly given her everything she had any right to expect. Then, because she had suddenly become unattainable, he was filled with a savage desire for her, and he started toward her.

She jumped back and picked up a stick of stovewood from the wood box. She tried to hit him, but he grabbed her arm, took the stick from her, and threw it away. He picked her up and carried her into the bedroom. She kicked and tried to bite him. But he slapped her hard across the face, and she cried out in pain. He threw her on the bed and lighted a lamp on the bureau. He pulled down the green blind at the window, but when he turned she jumped and ran toward the door. He caught her before she reached it, spun her around, and tore off her dress. He picked her up and carried her back to the bed. This time she lay there, all resistance gone.

Later, he didn't know how much later, he awoke and realized that she was not beside him. He was filled with a frantic worry, thinking she had left the house, and he got up and ran out of the bedroom. She was in the kitchen, staring at the charred cake she had been baking.

She must have heard him. Without turning, she said dully: "You ought to be happy now. You made me burn my cake."

He stared at her. Crazy! She was completely crazy! He said, quietly, "Come back to bed." She picked up the lamp from the kitchen table and went with him, docilely enough.

The next time he awoke, it was full daylight. He sat up and rubbed his eyes, smelling the coffee she was making. He was hungry, and she was getting breakfast for him. She'd get over her spell. Today he'd talk some sense into her. They'd plan their trip to Denver.

His clothes were scattered on the floor. He walked to the window and put the shade up. The sun was noon high. He was startled, not realizing he had slept so long. He yawned and ran a hand through his disheveled hair.

Then he saw his gun belt on the floor, the Colt still in holster, and he had a bad moment. The way she had felt last night, it was a wonder she hadn't killed him. He wouldn't take a chance like that again.

He was reaching for his clothes when he heard her run across the living room. He looked up to see her standing in the doorway, her slim body taut. She began to laugh, pointing a trembling finger at him, and he was angry, thinking she was ridiculing him.

"Did you think God would listen to me, Matt?" she said when she could stop laughing. "Of all the people in the world, did you think He would listen to *me?*"

She was out of her head. He said uneasily,

"What's the matter with you?"

"Nothing's the matter with me, but there's going to be something the matter with you in a minute. What I prayed for is happening."

Someone knocked on the front door, and she whirled toward it. It took a second for his mind, still foggy from sleep and weariness, fully to grasp the situation and the danger of discovery that faced him. Because of the way in which Betty was acting, he knew it wasn't Pollock or one of his men. Maybe it was Sullivan, who had said he wanted to buy the Manders place, but whoever it was he couldn't be found in the house with Betty Erdman.

She had almost reached the door when the momentary paralysis left him. He yanked his gun from its holster and lunged toward the bedroom door, screaming, "You let anybody in and I'll kill him!" She gave him a glance over her shoulder, smiling as a woman does who is squeezing all she can from a sweet moment of vengeance, then reached for the doorknob.

CHAPTER NINE

When Jim awoke, it was well into the morning.

He got up and washed his face, hands making a sandpapery sound against the dark stubble. Maylor had been too hasty the night before to give him a good shave. He was stiff, his back and side were sore, but his head had stopped aching.

Jim ate breakfast in the dining room of the hotel. He must be a pariah, he thought, judging by the actions of the waitress, who rushed away the instant she had his order. A few minutes later she brought his ham and eggs and hurried away again. He was aware of the covert glances the other customers gave him. When he left the hotel, the clerk was busy looking the other way. At the moment he was the most famous man in Bakeoven.

He went at once to the bank. The interior was as imposing as the granite exterior: an ornate crystal chandelier that seemed to Jim a waste of money, a marble-surfaced counter with intricate brass scrollwork around the teller's-window, and two expensive mahogany desks in the rear of the room, one of them holding a shiny gold name plate with the words *Matthew Seery* engraved upon it.

The back wall held a portrait of Matt's father much like the one Jim had seen the night before. Staring at the bold eyes and predatory nose, Jim wondered what it was like to be the son of a man like that. He put a hand on the edge of the marble counter, considering the implications of his thought.

Apparently Matt was the only child, a spoiled mother's pet at that. Alexander must have been a sort of pirate, building his empire from close to nothing, if Matt had told it right. If he was the man Jim judged him to be, he must have been sick with disappointment as he watched Matt grow up.

The teller was a banty of a man with a projecting upturned chin and a long nose that combined to give his face a sort of nutcracker look, an illusion that was increased by the fact that he had no teeth and was constantly sucking at his lips. He sat at a desk working on a ledger, covertly watching Jim and hoping Jim didn't know it.

"I want to see Matt Seery," Jim said.

"He won't be in today," the man said, still working on the ledger.

"Where is he?"

"I don't know."

Exasperated, Jim said, "In a minute I'll come back there and pry your nose loose from your chin and you'll talk me to death."

The man rose and laid down his pen. A diamond stickpin glittered in his tie. A gift from the Seery family, Jim thought. Part of the business of appearing prosperous, as bankers should appear.

"I know who you are, Sullivan," the man said in a loud voice, "but you're not intimidating one of Pollock's men now. You are in the Seery State Bank and you will show the proper respect."

The bold front wasn't enough to hide his fear. Jim said, "All right, I'll show you some respect," and started toward the swinging gate at the end of the counter.

"I think he's at the ranch," the man said, lips quivering like a butterfly's wings, "but he doesn't want to be disturbed."

"I want to see him about getting your job," Jim said.

He left the bank, laughing silently at the worried expression that suddenly flowed across the man's face. His chin had dropped so that he didn't look quite so much like a nutcracker as he had. Outside, Jim paused and rolled a smoke, looking up at the high south wall of the valley with its layers of red, yellow, and buff sandstone.

The thought struck Jim that even the granite bank building seemed insignificant beside such a work of nature. Now, with the sheltering night gone, Matt Seery's town seemed cheap and tawdry in the unrelenting morning sunlight. Alexander Seery must have hated the south wall every time he looked at it. It would have made him seem very small, even to himself, and Jim was sure that none of the Seerys wanted to appear small.

He finished his cigarette, but the street remained deserted and still. Not a single horse was at any of the hitch racks. There was not even a mongrel dog dozing in the deep red dust. Waiting, Jim thought. Or sleeping. Or scared, not knowing what Nate Pollock would do.

He had to see Seery today, before Troy got in town. Jess Darket might be the answer. Decision made, he strode to the livery stable and found Darket in the harness room.

Darket said: "Good morning, Sullivan. I

see you're able to be on your feet."

"I'm able," Jim said. "I want to see Matt Seery, and the yahoo over at the bank thought he might be at his ranch. I want you to ride out there with me. I might get lost."

Darket cocked his head and blew out a long breath, the tips of his mustache fluttering. "Why don't you tell the truth?"

Jim grinned. "All right. Since you're going to be Seery's father-in-law, you're pretty good insurance Pollock's boys will let me alone. I've got a hunch that even Pollock walks easy where any of the Seery family is concerned."

"Well, you're being honest and that's better." Darket picked up a handful of copper rivets and let them dribble through his fingers. "Why should I?"

"To keep me alive," Jim answered, "in case I change my mind about taking that star."

Darket studied Jim for a long moment, his head still cocked. "I've sure done some wondering about you, Sullivan." He rose. "All right, I'll go, only I won't guarantee anything about Nate Pollock. Town is one thing, but up there we'll be in his bailiwick."

Jim grinned at him again. "You know, Darket, facing danger is like facing the sun. It throws your shadow behind you. Let's ride."

■ ■ ■ ■

The morning was half spent when Jim left Bakeoven with Jess Darket. The town was aptly named, he thought. Even now, in early fall, the heat pressed down upon the valley like a heavy pall. There was no wind, just hot dry air trapped between the high, streaked sandstone walls that flanked the valley.

For the first time the idea came to Jim that there was more to Troy's idea of irrigating the valley than he had thought. The road followed the south wall, a thick growth of cedars adding a gray-green tinge to the talus slope. The valley floor sloped gently to Jim's right toward the creek that took a meandering course from the shoulder of Telescope Mountain to the river, willows making a thick screen along both banks.

From the road Jim could see that the valley was thinly settled. Probably the ranchers had homesteaded in it at about the time Alexander Seery had started the town of Bakeoven. Jim doubted that one-tenth of the valley was patented land.

Grass was knee-high on a horse, the bent heads heavy with seed. Jim had no idea how many head of cattle the ranchers owned, but they undoubtedly had some sort of self-established control that prevented the valley from being overgrazed during the winter months. Summer probably presented no problem. There should be ample grass on the mesas that lay on both sides of the valley and in the canyons and on the ridges of Telescope Mountain.

Two things about the valley impressed Jim. One was the fact that, lying here below these high rims, the valley would not have severe winters, and therefore the growing season would be relatively long. Probably it was one of the things that had appealed to the stockmen when they first saw the valley. The second thing that impressed Jim was the fertility of the red soil. The lush grass proved that.

This end of the valley was like nothing he had seen on the other side of the river. Not a ranch had been in sight when he had come down from the mesa, but now he could see half a dozen or more, lying along the creek two or three miles from the road. Likely there were more on the other side of the willows.

As they rode west, the valley grew narrower and the lift of the land became more pronounced. Near noon they swung north, Jim motioning to a group of log buildings tucked in a small cove in the southwest corner of the valley, the first ridge of Telescope Mountain rising directly behind it.

"Whose place is that?" Jim asked.

"Pollock's," Darket answered. "He has the biggest spread in the valley. There are just three outfits up here — or I should say two, Pollock's and Matt's. Pollock took over Manders' place after the old man was killed." Darket jerked his head at a small log house and a few outbuildings to their left. "That's Manders' place yonder."

As they rode past the house, Jim noticed a thin column of smoke standing motionless above the chimney, mute evidence that Betty Erdman had been brought back. They crossed the creek, hoofs making sharp echoing sounds on the planks of the narrow bridge. The stream was fair-sized, even this late in the season, full of clear water that chattered noisily as it ran swiftly over a rocky bottom between thick willow walls.

A quarter of a mile behind Manders' buildings an aspen-covered slope slanted up sharply from the floor of the valley, the creek gouging out a narrow channel before it leveled out to take its meandering course to the river. Up there somewhere behind that slope would be the reservoir site Troy had mentioned.

"Anybody ever talk about putting in a ditch system and a dam to hold back the spring run-off?" Jim asked.

Darket threw him a quick, questioning look. "We've all thought about it. Just thought. That's all."

"You're bound to have dry years," Jim said. "Looks like it would be a lifesaver."

Darket nodded. "It would. There have been years we had to sell young stuff we would have kept if we'd had grass to winter them. We'd have had grass if we'd had water to irrigate. Now you want to know what's stopping us. The answer is one man. Pollock."

"Bound to come," Jim said, "whether Pollock wants it or not."

"Sure," Darket said sourly. "It'll come after Pollock is dead. Eight, nine years ago old man Manders was working on the idea, but he was shot. Maybe that was why. I dunno, but I do know one thing. A dam up here would fetch a lot of folks up on the mountain, and that's what Pollock doesn't want to happen. The way it is now, Pollock uses the mountain for summer range and nobody fools around up there. That's the way he wants it."

"Seery's ranch is here."

"Well, Matt don't worry Pollock on account of he uses Starlight Mesa for summer range. That's southeast of here."

"What you're saying is that Pollock killed Manders to keep the dam from being built. That it?"

Darket stared straight ahead. "No, I didn't say that. At the time they claimed Manders was killed by outlaws." He swung off the road to follow a short lane. "This is Matt's place. He must be around. That's his chestnut yonder in the corral."

If Jim had drawn a picture of what he guessed Matt Seery's ranch would be, he would not have missed it by far. The house was a square stone structure that might have been built for a fort. The other buildings were made of logs. Two ancient cottonwoods in front of the house laid a welcome shade across the hitch pole. Everything was neat and clean, and the corral poles were painted white. Order would be Seery's first rule, Jim thought as he stepped down.

"I'll wait here," Darket said. "Matt's probably inside."

Jim looped the reins around the pole and walked up the path to the door. He knocked, and when there was no answer, knocked again, louder this time. Still no answer. He circled the house, following a trail through the tall grass. Apparently the place was deserted most of the summer. Even the path showed little sign of use.

Jim hammered on the back door, but still he could not rouse anyone. Uneasiness began working in Jim. Seery couldn't be far away, or his horse wouldn't be in the corral. Jim glanced at the woodpile. A double-bitted ax had been driven into the chopping block, its edge rusty from a recent rain. Obviously no one had used it for weeks.

Jim returned to the hitch rack. "Can't raise anybody. Seery wouldn't walk off and leave his horse, would he?"

"He's no more of a walker than you or me as long as he's got a horse." Darket stroked his mustache, frowning, worry growing in him. "It doesn't look good, Sullivan. I never did cotton to the notion of him living so close to Pollock, but he's too stubborn to sell. I've told him a dozen times that he'd stumble onto something Pollock didn't want him to see and he'd get plugged."

"Why? I mean, what would he see?"

"Might be anything. Pollock pretends to be a rancher, but he doesn't need toughs like Bert Knoll and Ace Rush to nurse cows. I figure he's an outlaw, and I'm not the only one that thinks it." He shrugged. "But hell, thinking and proving are two different things."

Darket studied the barn and bunkhouse, pulling thoughtfully at his mustache. Jim, watching him, sensed that Darket completely trusted Seery, and now was concerned about him. Suddenly Darket yanked his Winchester from the scabbard and stepping down, tied his horse.

"Maybe we'd better look around," Jim said.

"I was thinking the same," Darket said. "Been a lot of talk that Pollock steals a few head of steers when he has a chance and drives them up here onto the mountain. If Matt stumbled onto something like that, Pollock would kill him."

"Why don't you and your neighbors take a look up there?"

"It's a big country, and there's plenty of places to hide a small herd. Or hide a body, for that matter. We aren't real brave, Sullivan, if you want an honest answer. We'd rather lose some cattle now and then than get plugged."

Darket started across the yard to the bunkhouse. He went on: "Most of us just want to get along, and that means we steer clear of Pollock, but a lot of funny things have happened. Like not having a deputy.

Looks like Pollock might have a lot of influence somewhere. I suppose that some day we're going to have to organize and run Pollock and his whole damned bunch out of the valley."

Darket opened the bunkhouse door, glanced in, and then shut the door. He strode toward the corral and stood looking at the chestnut. Jim, coming to stand beside Darket, sensed that worry was growing in him, but whether it was concern for his own safety or fear for Seery was a question in Jim's mind. In town Jess had carried enough weight to get Pollock's men out of town, but here, as he had said before they left Bakeoven, he was on Pollock's home ground.

"Better look in the barn," Jim said.

"Yeah," Darket agreed reluctantly. "I don't like the looks of things, Sullivan. That horse hasn't been ridden for a spell. Matt may have come out last night and poked his nose right into a slug."

Jim strode toward the barn, Darket following slowly, as if their search was a chore he would rather avoid. He expected to find Seery's body, Jim thought, and maybe he was wishing his daughter had got herself married to Seery before this had happened.

Lifting the peg, Jim took hold of the hasp

and pulled the door open. He caught the musty barn smell, and in that same instant saw the two saddled horses tied in the stalls. He swore softly, not understanding, and felt Darket's hand grip his arm.

"That's Pollock's sorrel," Darket whispered. "The bay belongs to Ace Rush. He was one of the hellions who was working you over last night."

Jim stood motionless, a step outside the door. This was crazy, he thought. If Pollock's and Rush's horses were here, the men had to be here, too. Probably they had been in the house, watching him and remaining silent, knowing that if they had cut him down Darket would get away. Or, and this seemed more likely, Seery was in the house with Pollock and Rush, and they didn't want Darket to know.

"I don't savvy this," Jim said. "I'm going back to the house."

"I don't savvy, either," Darket said, "but you're not going to the house and get your head blowed off. We'll just mosey back to the horses and ride to town. We'll round up a posse, and if we find Matt's body Pollock's a dead duck."

"You ride to town," Jim said. "I'm going into the house."

He swung around, leaving the barn door

open. He had taken only one step when a man called: "Hoist 'em, gents. You ain't going into the house, Sullivan."

CHAPTER TEN

Jim wheeled to face the man who stood in the barn door, right hand poised over gun butt, but he didn't draw. He was looking into the muzzle of a cocked .45. The fellow was medium-tall and stocky, with red-flecked eyes that blinked as he stared into the sharp sunlight. Judging from the ugly expression on his wide bronzed face, it would take very little to make him pull the trigger.

The thought flashed through Jim's mind that the man had been in the gloomy interior of the barn and that it would take a moment before his eyes became accustomed to the sunlight. Darket had turned, too, his rifle on the ready, but he was afraid to move. The man repeated in an ominous tone, "Hoist 'em, gents."

"Where's Matt, Rush?" Darket demanded.

Rush's gaze was on Darket now. He started to say, "I don't know —" when Jim lunged at him.

It was a crazy gamble, but judging from what had happened last night Jim knew he could expect no mercy from Pollock's crew. He had a choice of risking death now, or being sure of it later on. He had a chance. Not much, but a chance, and his gamble paid off.

Rush fired, the bullet slicing through Jim's coat along his right side. He felt the white-hot burn of the slug, but he wasn't badly hurt. Before Rush could fire again, he batted the gun barrel down with his left, his right swinging up in a short, vicious blow to Rush's chin.

Pollock's man gave ground, his head swiveled half around, his second bullet kicking up a geyser of red dust, and Jim hit him again in the face. Rush sprawled backward into the barn litter, and Jim jumped on him, knees hammering into the fellow's belly and bringing a yeasty groan from him. He cracked him on one side of the face and then the other, vaguely aware that Darket was yelling: "Get off him, Sullivan, and I'll shoot him! Get off!"

But there was no getting off Ace Rush. The man's great arms circled Jim and hugged him, drawing him down as closely as if they were roped together. He was fighting by sheer instinct, for the first two blows Jim had landed would have knocked out an ordinary man. But Rush was no ordinary man; he had the strength of a bull. His big hands pressed against Jim's spine, and for an instant Jim thought Rush would break his back.

Darket was dancing around, still yelling for Jim to get off. Almost hysterical, he was a greater menace than Rush. Jim was on top. Somehow he raised a knee and drove it downward into Rush's crotch. The man cried out in agony, his grip relaxing enough for Jim to break free.

Jim staggered to his feet, calling to Darket, "Don't shoot." He was between Darket and Rush, and at the moment Darket had no chance to fire, but Jim was off balance and still laboring for breath. Rush, flat on his back, rammed a boot into Jim's stomach and knocked him flat. He fell dangerously close to the hind foot of the sorrel in one of the stalls. The horse kicked, the hoof missing Jim's head by a fraction of an inch. Jim rolled back across the runway, and when he regained his feet he saw that Darket was standing over Rush, the rifle barrel lined on the man's belly.

"Don't shoot!" Jim shouted. "He won't be any good to us dead."

"I'm going to let him have it," Darket gritted. "He's a damned back-shooting bastard. I'm going to kill him."

Jim got to him in time, twisting the rifle out of Darket's hands. He said: "Cool down. If Pollock's in the house, he'd plug us before we could get to the horses."

Darket stumbled back to lean against the barn wall, breathing hard, sanity returning to him. He stared bleakly at Jim, who was covering Rush with the rifle, and nodded, finally understanding. "I guess that's right," he muttered, "but if he don't tell us what happened to Matt I'll kill him anyhow."

He wasn't carrying a belt gun, so Jim didn't know what he planned to use to kill Rush with, but it didn't matter. Darket was still too excited to think straight. He must think a lot of Matt Seery, Jim thought.

Rush sat up and wiped blood and sweat from his face. He had dropped his gun, and he stared at it longingly, tempted to make a try for it. Jim said, "You reach for that iron, and I'll plug you." Rush slowly got to his feet and glared at Jim, blood dribbling from his nose and spreading along his upper lip. He licked his lip and called Jim a name.

"Talk," Darket raged. "Where's Matt?"

Rush spat out a mouthful of blood. He said, "I don't know."

Rush retreated to the back wall and stood against it, eyes swinging from Jim to Darket and back to Jim. Darket picked up a pitchfork. He said, "I've never killed a man, but I will now if you don't talk."

"We ain't seen Seery," Rush muttered. "We've been waiting for him. Hell, you know as much about him as we do."

"Why in hell would you be waiting for him?" Darket demanded.

"Dunno. That's Pollock's business. He's in the house."

"They're waiting to kill him," Darket breathed. "There ought to be a rope around here, Sullivan. Let's swing this bastard."

"Does being a mayor make you judge and jury to boot?" Jim asked.

Darket threw the pitchfork down and swore. "Well, what *will* we do with him?"

Jim knew that it was of no use to tell Darket that Seery and Pollock had been working together. He simply wouldn't believe it. But Seery was around somewhere, and Jim decided that the only other place he could be was Manders' house. He held his answer to Darket's question for a moment, turning it over in his mind. He could take Darket to Manders' house and find Seery with Betty Erdman if he was guessing right, but it wouldn't buy him a thing and he'd lose any chance he had of making Seery trust him.

"We'll let him go," Jim said finally, "if he can think of some way to get Pollock out of the house."

Rush cried, "I'll get him out of the house if you'll give me your word we can go."

"You don't know my word's any good," Jim said.

"You kept that son of a bitch from plugging me," Rush said. "I'll take your word."

Darket didn't like Jim's plan. He picked up the pitchfork again and leaned on the handle. "You're a fool, Sullivan. They'll double cross us."

"They'll be dead if they try it," Jim said. "Darket, I've been thinking I'll take that marshal's star if you'll go to the county seat and get me a deputy's badge to go with it. A man needs both if he's going to do any good."

Bewildered by Jim's unexpected switch, Jess said, "If Matt couldn't get a deputy —"

"Being mayor, you'll carry weight," Jim urged. "Will you try it?"

Darket was silent for a long moment, jabbing the pitchfork into the manure and straw that covered the runway and lifting it and jabbing again. He still believed that Seery had been murdered, but he was thinking about what had happened last night in town. Because he wanted Pollock punished legally, he finally nodded.

"All right," Darket said. "But I don't savvy why you've changed your mind or why you're out here."

"It's too long a yarn to tell now," Jim said. "Go ahead, Rush. Get Pollock out of the house, but if you make a run for it you'll get a slug in the back."

Rush walked toward the door, eyeing Darket as he passed as if afraid he'd get the pitchfork in his ribs. When he reached the door, he called, "I've got 'em, Nate." He stepped back and moved into a stall. "He'll come." He remained there, staring malevolently at Darket.

"He's still afraid he's going to die," Jim said. "Looks like he's not ready."

"Is a man ever ready?" Darket cried passionately. "Was Bob Jarvis ready last night?"

"We'll get Bert Knoll for that," Jim said. "You know, Maylor, folks get just about what they deserve. You people have let Pollock run roughshod over you for years. Letting Jarvis die last night was part of this whole thing."

"Yeah," Darket muttered. "We'll all fry in hell because of it."

A moment later Pollock stood in the doorway, staring at the rifle in Jim's hand.

Jim said, "So you're Nate Pollock."

"That's who I am right enough." Pollock laughed, a great laugh that rumbled from deep inside him. "Yes, sir, that's who I am."

He was a huge man in his early forties, gross and ungainly his belly bulging over crossed cartridge belts. He was dirty, and a week's stubble darkened his heavy face. Pale eyes, almost hidden behind great rolls of fat, were bold and challenging. He looked soft, but he wasn't. Jim judged there was more hard meat in his body than blubber.

"Drop your gun belts," Jim said.

Pollock's gaze flicked to Rush's face. "So you got 'em, did you, Ace? If I had a minute alone with you, I'd —"

"You'll get it," Jim said. "I promised Rush you two would ride out of here. I just wanted you to know I'm Matt Seery's friend."

"Mister, that don't cut no ice with me," Pollock said. "Not out here. In town it would be different. You're a tough boy, redhead, real tough, so I reckon you're lying about being Seery's friend. He don't like tough hands."

"No, I'm not lying," Jim said. "I'm wondering how smart you are."

Pollock's deep laugh rumbled out of him, his belly shaking. He was enjoying himself,

Jim thought. Some men, like Seery, were deceptive and hard to judge. Others, like Ace Rush, had a veneer of toughness that was easily stripped from them. But Pollock was neither. He was utterly vicious, without the redeeming qualities that could be found even in a man like Gabe Dykens. Now that he had seen him, Jim could understand how he had been able to intimidate the valley.

Pollock shoved big thumbs under his belt and rocked back on his heels. He asked, as if amused, "Meaning what, Red?"

"I've got second sight," Jim answered. "If you don't get out of the valley while you can, you're a dead man."

"Well now, you've cut quite a swath since you hit this country. You beefed Perkins and you winged Knoll. From the looks of Ace's face, you worked him over. But me, I'm a bigger caliber." He tapped his barrel of a chest. "I'm Nate Pollock, bucko. I run the valley, and I aim to stay."

"All right, you stay and I'll help bury you," Jim said. "I told you to unbuckle your gun belts."

Pollock obeyed, then walked into the stall that held his sorrel and backed him into the runway. Rush threw a glance at Jim, a little hesitant now, as if afraid of Pollock and not sure whether he was any better off if he left.

His eyes swung on around to Darket, and all doubt left him. He got his horse and joined Pollock outside the barn.

Jim handed the rifle to Darket, saying, "Take it easy."

Darket, watching Pollock and Rush ride down the lane to the county road, said: "You've got a soft spot, Sullivan. Some day it'll kill you."

Startled, Jim realized he'd had the same notion about Troy. You put two soft spots together and you have a fatal weakness, but Darket was wrong about him. This was a matter of judgment, not weakness.

"You head back to town," Jim said. "I'm going to visit Betty Erdman."

He saw Darket's face go dark and bitter, for the man was like many righteous people, unbending in his judgment of women like Betty Erdman. He said harshly: "A man has only one reason for visiting a wanton like her. You'll make Pollock hate you more than ever."

"That's impossible," Jim said, impatient now. "How long will it take you to go to the county seat and get back?"

"Three or four days. It's a long ride from here to Placerville where I catch the narrow gauge. Be a longer ride if I go over the Divide."

"Get moving," Jim said. "I want that deputy's badge."

"You're singing a different tune," Darket murmured. "If the Erdman woman has anything to do with —"

"She hasn't." Jim started toward the horses in front of the house. When Darket caught up with him, Jim added, "I aim to run Pollock's bunch out of the valley. I need to be deputy to make it legal."

They mounted, Darket saying nothing until they had ridden down the lane. Then he said: "I'm taking the long way back to town so I won't go past Pollock's ranch. You'd better come with me."

"I'll be along after a while."

Darket reined up and pulled at his mustache, studying Jim. He said: "I'll be responsible for you if I get a deputy's badge. I don't know about this, Sullivan. You may be an outlaw."

Though Jim was infuriated, he controlled his voice. "You'd better remember what just happened. You were the one who wanted to take the law into your own hands, and I kept you from it."

Shame was in Darket then. He said, with sudden humility, "Yes, I should have remembered." He raised a hand again to pull at his mustache, a nervous gesture clearly

151

indicating his worry and indecision. "But I still don't know about Matt. We ought to . . ."

"I think he's alive and I think I can find him." Jim swung his roan toward Manders' house and then pulled up again. "Darket, what did Manders' neighbors think of him?"

"Why, we liked and respected him," Darket said. "Everyone but Pollock. If Manders hadn't been killed, we'd have had that dam a long time ago. Since then Pollock has controlled this end of the valley so that even Matt hasn't bucked him." Darket frowned, his thoughts going back across the years, then he added: "Now that I think of it, Manders was a sort of prophet. He said if we didn't work together, we'd see this valley bathed in blood. Looks like it'll happen if we don't get Pollock out of here."

Jim nodded. The dam, then, would still be built if Troy could be made to see it. He said, "So long," and turned his horse south toward the Manders house, his mind fixed on Troy. He wondered what she was thinking, now that she was almost home.

Was she remembering her father as Darket remembered him? Was she recalling what he believed in, what he had taught her? Or had it all been lost in her nine-year absence, burned out in the bitterness and smoldering passion for revenge that had so completely guided everything she had done?

As Jim dismounted in front of the Manders house and tied, he told himself that his happiness was bound up with Troy's, and that their future was bound up with that of the valley. Both hung on the answers to the questions he had asked himself. Only time would bring the answers.

Jim hesitated, seeing no sign of life around the place except the smoke that rose from the chimney. There was still no wind; the air was oven-hot, smelling of dust and the sage that grew tall enough behind the house to hide a man on horseback. He had never seen sagebrush grow to such tree-like proportions, and he was struck by this further proof of the fertility of the red soil.

He walked up the path thinking that Seery wouldn't be happy to see him, but it seemed to be the only thing he could do. Now that he was here, he was determined to have a look at the reservoir site, and Seery could show him and keep Pollock's hardcase crew off his neck.

He knocked, and the door swung open at once. Betty Erdman stood there, her slender body taut with expectancy, smiling as if she had a secret reason for being amused. She said, "Come in, Mr. Sullivan," her voice quite loud, and stepped back so that she was out of the doorway.

Jim hesitated, vaguely warned by the strange expression of anticipation on the girl's face, then, disregarding the prickle that ran along his spine, he stepped into the house. He heard Matt Seery scream an oath at him; he wheeled toward the sound of the voice, and saw Seery standing there, completely naked, a gun in his hand.

He needed only the one glance to tell him that Seery was out of his head with fear or rage, or both. He grabbed for his .45, but before it cleared leather Betty was clinging to his arm, crying, "No, no!"

He tried desperately to shake her loose, but could not. He saw Seery's gun come up, saw the hideous expression on the man's pale face. As he struggled to free himself of the girl's tenacious grip, time seemed to stop and become eternity while he waited to die.

CHAPTER ELEVEN

Seery's long white arm straightened in front of him, the gun pointed at Jim's chest; he pulled the trigger, but there was no explosion. Just the click of the hammer dropping on an empty. Seery looked at the gun, blinking, befuddled by its failure.

"I took the loads out of your gun last night," the girl screamed. "I had a gun. I was going to kill you myself today, but I saw Sullivan coming. I — I —"

She began to cry. Releasing her grip on Jim's arm, she ran into the kitchen and slammed the door. Jim drew his gun and walked slowly toward Seery, who for the moment seemed incapable of either speech or movement. Frenzy had driven him to the point of murdering Jim, but the moment was gone, and he began to tremble.

"You're out of your head, mister," Jim said. "I figured you were here, and when I come in to find out why you weren't in the bank you try to kill me. Are we making a deal or not?"

Seery threw his gun across the room, swearing bitterly. "You don't understand. That girl —"

"No, I don't understand for a fact," Jim broke in. "I met your fiancée last night, and it sure as hell wasn't Betty Erdman."

"Put your gun up," Seery said wearily, and walked into the bedroom. "There won't be any more trouble."

Jim stood in the doorway, a lean shoulder against the jamb. He'd met up with some crazy people, but Matt Seery seemed the craziest. Matt had made a fool of himself, the one thing which he could never forget. Prestige, power, and a sense of his superiority had always artificially buoyed a man who would otherwise have drowned in the sea of his own ineptitude.

Seery sat on the edge of the bed and held his head, completely humiliated. Jim, watching him through a long, taut moment of silence, sensed that Seery would always hate him for what had just happened. Inadvertently he had lost any chance of accomplishing what Troy had sent him to do, but he would continue to try, at least until Troy reached Bakeoven.

Seery stirred and rubbed his face with

both hands. He began to dress, avoiding Jim's eyes. He said: "I'm not myself this morning, Sullivan. I hope you'll overlook what happened. It was just that I — I didn't expect you." He buttoned his shirt, fingers slow and awkward. "I haven't had time to think about your proposition. Too many things have happened since I saw you."

"Mostly that you found out Betty tried to leave the valley, wasn't it?"

Seery nodded. "I owe you an explanation, although I realize no amount of explaining will satisfy you. It's true I am engaged to Lily Darket. She's the only girl in the valley my mother considers eligible. If I mentioned Betty, I'd be disinherited. I told you last night that this ranch is all I own personally."

While Seery dressed, Jim thought of what Troy had said about the man. It didn't make sense. Pollock, yes, but not Seery; yet Seery was the one who worried Troy. She had said Pollock could be handled, but Seery would be tough. How could Troy, who knew men so well, be as wrong as she had been with Matt Seery? Or had she been wrong? Only time would give Jim the answer.

"For years I've been two men," Seery continued, his face as lifeless as putty. "I've been the banker, a generous one. I've stood for something in this valley, the same things my mother stood for. Call it respectability if you want to, although the word is a lie. My other life has been here. I've loved Betty for a long time. I've done a great many things for her, and she repaid me by running away with the Jarvis boy. I told you you wouldn't understand. It doesn't make any difference except that you know something about me no one else knows. If you tell, you will not be believed."

Perhaps Seery was trying to justify himself in the eyes of a stranger, or perhaps he was trying to keep the road open to make the bargain Jim had offered last night. And there was a third possibility. Perhaps Seery was hoping to buy Jim's silence.

"I'm no blabbermouth," Jim said sharply. "Besides, if I ruined your reputation you'd be no help to me."

Seery sat down on the bed and tugged on his boots. "Blackmail, isn't it? I play your game, but you call the turn. If I refuse, you tell folks I've been keeping Betty."

"Blackmail's a dirty word," Jim said. "Let's say I want you for a partner."

Seery rose and put on his coat. "Why did you come here?"

"To get you to take me to the reservoir site the Manders girl said she owned. You were supposed to meet me at the bank."

"I had to come out here," Seery muttered, and started toward the door. "Let's see if she's got breakfast ready."

"I've got some things to tell you first," Jim said. "One is, you've got to get Pollock off my neck."

Seery was genuinely surprised. "You mean because you shot Perkins and wounded Knoll?"

"That's part of it." Jim told him about the beating he'd taken the night before, and his fight with Ace Rush. "I told Pollock to get out of the country. One thing is sure, Seery. We can't fetch settlers to a valley that's buffaloed by a hardcase like Nate Pollock."

"I'll talk to him," Seery said.

"And another thing. If we go into this deal, you've got to run the bank, not your mother. Judging by last night, I'd say you can't call your soul your own."

Seery flushed. "Leave my family troubles to me, Sullivan."

"Glad to, but I want your help. The way things stand now, it won't work."

"No, I guess it won't." Seery left the bedroom and crossed the living room to the kitchen. "Breakfast ready?"

"It's ready," Betty said dully. "Tell Sullivan I put a plate on for him."

"Sullivan, you want to eat?" Seery called.

Jim had paused in the living room, wondering if Troy had left the house as it was now. At one time the furniture had been expensive: a black leather couch, heavy oak table, red plush chair, and a bookcase filled with books. They were the kind of furniture Troy's father would have bought, Jim thought. Probably Seery had simply installed Betty here, leaving the house the way Troy had left it.

"Sullivan," Seery called.

"Coming," Jim said, and went on into the kitchen.

Seery had started to eat. Jim sat down across from him, and Betty brought the coffeepot from the stove. Now, seeing her in daylight, he discovered she was even prettier than he had thought. She had taken pains with her hair, and she was wearing a pink gingham dress with a tight-fitting bodice that snugged her round breasts and tiny waist.

There was no talk for a time, Betty standing at the big range with her back to the men. Presently she brought another platter of flapjacks to the table, asking, "This going to be enough?"

"Sure, sure," Seery said impatiently.

Jim, glancing at the girl, saw the same sadness in her poignant face that he had seen the night before. He wondered about it. She wasn't grieving for Jarvis, whose death she had caused, Jim thought. And though she had planned to kill Seery — or so she had said — when the time came she had kept Jim from shooting him.

"I don't savvy this," Jim said. "You had it all set up, but in the pinch you wouldn't let me plug Seery."

"Shut up," Seery said harshly, "and stay out of my business."

"I don't savvy, either," Betty said, ignoring Seery. "I just couldn't let it happen. That's all. Maybe it was because there was a time when I worshiped Matt, but he was always ashamed of me. I thought he'd change, but he never did. When I went to town, Matt wouldn't even speak to me." She threw out a hand toward Jim, eyes begging for his understanding. "I've got to get out of this valley. Will you help me?"

"And be another Jarvis?" Jim asked.

She whirled and went back to the stove. Seery said: "She's had everything. She had no call to go with Jarvis."

Jim finished his coffee and rose. Last night the girl had had his sympathy, but not now. She had used Jarvis and had led him to his death, but her sorrow was for herself, not him. She must have come here willingly, Jim thought. Now she could take what she got.

As he walked toward the living room, Betty cried out, "Sullivan, take me with you!" When he kept on, she screamed: "He hasn't given me everything. He's lying."

Seery got up and kicked back his chair. "What have you lacked?"

"A decent life," she cried. "Marriage. A home. You promised."

Without another word to her, Seery followed Jim into the front room. He said, "I'll saddle up and we'll take a look at that reservoir site."

Seery picked up his Colt and went into the bedroom. He came out a moment later, buckling his gun belt around him, the .45 in its holster. Jim said, "If you figure to use that gun to shut my mouth . . ."

"I don't," Seery said. "If what you said last night is true, we'll make the deal."

Seery took his hat off the antlers that hung near the door and left the house, walking fast. Jim paused, looking back at the girl who stood in the kitchen doorway, her hands clenched at her sides. She said, "Don't trust him, Sullivan."

"Why are you telling me that?" Jim asked.

"You tried to help last night," she said

miserably. "It's the least I can do."

He left then, and mounting, rode slowly toward Seery's ranch, Seery striding along the road in front of him. What a hell of a twist this was, Jim thought, and wished Troy was here. What would she do with Betty when she found the girl in her house?

Jim put the question out of his mind. That would be her problem, not his. His eyes swung east to follow the long trough of the valley sheltered between the high, varicolored walls. Troy was coming back for revenge. She was wrong. He had told her that, but would she see it, once she was back?

He reined up in the shade of the cottonwoods in front of Seery's house, his mind turning inward. He had never been satisfied with himself from the day he had left home. He had thought the mere leaving would be enough, but he had been wrong. He had known and envied men who had found peace of mind, content with the day at hand. He wondered, Would he find that peace here, with Troy? Or was she little better than Betty Erdman, who had callously used Bob Jarvis? If he lost his life, would Troy take his death as lightly as Betty took Jarvis's?

It was an ugly thought, and it soured his mind. He watched Seery open the corral gate and heard him whistle. The chestnut lifted his head, whinnied, and came trotting to Seery, who patted his neck. Seery made no effort to hide the pleasure he felt as the horse nuzzled him.

A strange man, Matt Seery. Jim remembered how he had caressed the kitten the night before. He was hungry for love, as any man was, and perhaps there had been a time when he and Betty had found that love in each other.

Seery saddled and mounted, motioning to Jim, who left the patch of shade and rode into the glaring sunlight. They angled southwest toward the creek. A quarter of a mile from the house, Seery said: "If you're an engineer, you can start figuring on how a ditch would have to go. I've had this same idea myself, but I lacked the capital, so it never got any further than the idea."

"The bank could —"

"My mother's bank," Seery reminded him. "I take orders the same as any man. We couldn't fool her by using the bank to gain possession of the patented land. That's the weakness of your scheme."

It was a weakness in Troy's plan she could not have foreseen because she had not understood the relationship between Matt Seery and his mother. Nothing could come from the scheme, and Seery undoubtedly realized it. Still, he had not said so. He must, Jim thought, have an angle of his own, and Jim remembered with some uneasiness that Betty had warned him not to trust Seery.

They swung directly west, following a line of cedar posts that once had formed the fence between the Seery and Manders ranches, but the wire had been removed long ago. They began to climb through the aspens, on which the leaves were already turning gold. Hoofs rattled in the dry grass and fallen leaves as they picked a path through the white trees. Half an hour later they reached the top of the ridge, threaded their way down a sharp, rocky cliff, and presently reached a small park that was in a bowl set on the mountain slope.

"This is it." Seery pointed at the stream that meandered across the park and disappeared down a narrow, rock-choked gorge. "Wouldn't take a big dam."

"How good is the rock? A dam's no good if the sides leak."

Seery hipped around in the saddle and gave him a searching stare. "How much do you know about the Manders girl and her father?"

Suspicion was plain to read in the banker's

pale face. Jim said: "I told you last night. I talked to her in No Man's Land. She thought I was a drifter, which I was at the time, just poking around. I don't know a damn' thing for sure except that she was figuring on coming back. I'm not even sure of that. Just talk, maybe."

"How much would you pay?"

"No more than I have to. Looks like two ditches, one on each side of the valley. Take a lot of money."

"Last night I heard some big talk about a million dollars."

Jim gave him a wry grin. "A banker ought to know that a millionaire gets to be a millionaire by shaving a nickel off every dime. Too much construction expense will stop the deal before it starts."

"You've had your look," Seery said. "Let's go back."

They swung around and put their horses up the steep grade. They stopped on top to let their horses blow, Jim looking westward at the mountain that lifted its massive bulk toward the sky. He said, "You didn't answer my question about the rock."

"Old man Manders said it was good," Seery said. "I think he knew. He was a dreamer, but he was smart, too."

"He made some tests?"

Seery nodded. "Wanted this to be a community enterprise, with all hands helping to build the dam and ditch and share the water." Seery shrugged. "He got killed before he could get it started."

They rode through the cool shade of the aspens and came again into the glare of the sun. Jim said carefully, "I think I could make a tentative offer of fifty thousand for the Manders ranch if we got a sound title."

"I can arrange it," Seery said, without explaining what he had in mind.

There was no more talk as they turned along the country road toward Manders' house. As they passed it, Seery stared straight ahead. Jim wondered what would happen to Betty, and if Seery would still want her. She didn't like the life she had now, but if Seery turned her over to Pollock she would have an infinitely worse one.

The road made a turn at Pollock's lane, and a vague uneasiness nagged at Jim as he remembered that Jess Darket had been afraid to pass Pollock's on his way to town. Jim had far more to fear than Darket, for what had started in town would not be ended until Pollock and Rush and Knoll were dead, or Jim was.

At one moment there was no sound except the thud of hoofs against the dust-covered surface of the road; at the next the crack of rifles broke apart the stillness and the air was alive with bullets, one of them tugging at Jim's hat.

Cursing, Seery wheeled his horse. He yelled: "Ride, you fool. I'll stop it if I can."

Jim cracked steel to his roan, bending low over the saddle. Glancing back, he saw Seery ride toward Pollock's ranch, waving at them to stop firing. There was no more shooting, but Jim did not pull his horse down until he was out of rifle range. He had made a mistake about Matt Seery. He had discounted the man's courage: it took guts to ride directly into the face of that rifle fire. Pollock might be his friend, but a friend like that was about as dependable as a pet cougar.

CHAPTER TWELVE

Matt Seery was in a cold rage when he reined up in front of Pollock's ranch house and swung down. One of the bullets had come alarmingly close, close enough to slice a notch in the brim of his Stetson.

Pollock stood in the doorway, a rifle held in the crook of his arm, amusement showing on his moon-like face. Seery shouted: "What the hell do you mean, shooting at us like that? You might have hit me."

Pollock's great belly shook with a burst of laughter. "Now, Mr. Seery, you don't doubt our shooting talents, do you?"

Seery yanked off his hat and pointed at the bullet notch. "What does that look like?"

"Like good shooting, Mr. Seery. Real good shooting."

Seery put his hat on, taken aback by Pollock's bald effrontery. More than once during the last year he'd had an uneasy feeling that his control over Pollock was not so complete as it had been, that Pollock was making sly threats just as he had done now. But nothing had changed, and Seery had put it out of his mind because there seemed to be no reason for Pollock to become rebellious.

"I'd rather think it was bad shooting," Seery said.

His anger died in him. He found it hard to remain angry with Pollock. The man seemed good-natured most of the time; at least he was always able to laugh, whether he was telling an obscene joke or cracking a man's neck with his hands. More than that, he had done everything Seery required of him, even to keeping an eye on Betty Erdman, seeing she had plenty of grub, and protecting Seery's reputation by bragging in the Bakeoven saloon that he bedded down twice a week with Betty and that you couldn't find a better sleeping partner in any of the fancy houses in Denver.

Pollock was slow in stepping out of the doorway, the laughter leaving his face. Again the vague feeling of uneasiness swept over Seery. Then Pollock moved aside, saying, "Come in, Mr. Seery."

It was one of the incongruities of their relationship that Pollock and his men insisted on calling him "Mr. Seery." He often wished they would use his first name, as they did with one another, but they seemed to take perverse pleasure in keeping him out of their inner circle and treating him with synthetic respect.

Now, as he dropped into one of Pollock's homemade chairs, Seery was plagued by a premonition that his verbal contract with the outlaw pack was about to be canceled. He got his pipe out of his pocket and filled it, looking around the barren room with its log walls and puncheon floor and crude furniture. Pollock had never cared about creature comforts. He didn't have a comfortable chair in the place.

Bert Knoll stood by the window, left arm in a sling. He asked sourly, "How'd you get hooked up with that hombre?"

Seery took a moment to light his pipe before he answered. He sensed the bitterness of their temper. Even Pollock, who remained standing by the door, gave him a narrow-eyed, wicked stare, his face stripped of the good nature which was usually there when he was with Seery.

Ace Rush sat on a bench across the room, his face showing the beating Jim Sullivan had given him. A Mexican boy, Rafael Tafoya, stood leaning against the wall a few feet from Rush. He should have been with the roundup crew back on the mountain, and Seery wondered why he was there, then put it out of his mind.

"Sullivan came to Bakeoven to see me," Seery said. "He's an engineer representing a million dollars of Eastern capital. He's interested in a reservoir site, and I showed him the one on the Manders property this afternoon."

"He's a damned liar," Knoll flung at Seery. "He's a gunslinger. No engineer could throw lead like he did last night."

Seery shook his head. "He's carrying more gold on him than a hired gunhand would have, and he doesn't talk like a fiddle-footed tough. I think he's on the level."

"He's a dead man," Knoll said in a low tone. "I don't care whether he's on the level or not; he's a dead man."

"I know how you feel," Seery said, "but you can wait a few days. He said he'd give fifty thousand for the Manders place. Fifty thousand is worth waiting for."

"How are you going to get title to the Manders place?" Pollock asked.

"I can rig a deed that will look good," Seery said. "Good enough to make him send for his money, anyhow. That's as far as it needs to go, if you'll give me a hand. We'll see it never gets to Bakeoven."

"Fifty thousand is ten times what a man would pay for any spread in the valley," Pollock said. "A smart man like you ought to see that."

"Sure it's too much," Seery agreed, "but Sullivan knows the land holds the only reservoir site in the valley. And I'm familiar enough with Eastern investors to be certain that if I can convince Sullivan a fortune can be made in this valley, he'll pay that figure."

Pollock shrugged. "All right. If you're so damned certain, we'll wait, but there's another thing we ain't waiting on. You're getting rid of the Erdman girl. She ain't getting hold of no more of my boys like she done Bob Jarvis."

Seery rose and dropped his pipe into his pocket. It was the first time Pollock had ever tried to give him an order. Now, meeting the big man's cold stare, Seery realized that his feeling of impending trouble, which had been vague and intangible, was taking definite shape. But it would not do to show weakness.

"I'll make some other arrangement as soon as I can." Seery moved to the door. "By the way, Nate, my mother refuses to let me handle your business as I have in the past. You'll have to make a payment on your notes this fall."

It was a lie. His mother had never been concerned about Pollock's growing debt to the bank. At least she had never indicated that she was, although Seery suspected that the time would come when she'd use the debt to force Pollock out of the valley. Seery had said it simply to remind Pollock that he held the upper hand, but his ruse didn't work.

Pollock's great laugh rolled out of him. He said: "I don't reckon I will, Mr. Seery. You're going to tear those notes up."

Shocked, Seery said: "You know I can't do that. You owe the bank more than twenty thousand."

"I figure you will." Pollock motioned to the chair where Seery had been sitting. "Put your butt down there again, Mr. Seery. Rafe fetched in some news. If you ain't sitting down when you hear it, you'll fall down."

Seery obeyed, automatically reaching for his pipe and filling it. Whatever the news was, it was bad, or Pollock wouldn't be talking so big. He said, "I'm listening, but nothing can change the fact that you owe the bank twenty thousand dollars."

"Oh, hell," Knoll shouted, exasperated, "tell him, Nate. I want to see his face."

"I'll tell him," Pollock said harshly. "My boys have finished roundup, and they'll have

174

the beef herd in the valley in a couple of days. I sent Rafe to your cow camp to see if your boys could throw your herd in with ours after we cross the river. Tell him what you found, Rafe."

"You have no beef herd, Señor Seery," Tafoya said. "The pasture gate was down and the steers were gone. Your cabin was burned." He shuddered, thinking about what he had found. "I kicked around in the ashes. Three skulls. Your boys must have been burned alive."

The pipe fell from Seery's mouth. He caught it before it reached the floor. As he stared at the young Mexican, he began to tremble. A thing like that could not have happened to him. But he couldn't doubt Tafoya.

"Your steers are in New Mexico by now," Pollock said. "When we get back from Placerville, I'll send Rafe and a couple of the boys to round up your cows and young stuff, providing you burn them notes. If you think you can manage without us, go right ahead."

"I'll see," Seery whispered. "I'll see."

He rose and walked out of the house, lurching like a drunken man. He mounted, knowing Pollock had him. It would be impossible to get any of the small cowmen to ride for him. By the time the pool herd had been shipped and they had driven their she-stuff down to the valley, snow would be two feet deep on Starlight Mesa.

He saw that Pollock had followed him out of the house. He asked: "What's happened, Nate? We've always got along, always worked together. But today . . ."

His voice trailed off. Pollock might have been a stranger, for his fat face showed none of the good nature that had always been so much in evidence when Seery was with him. Contempt was there to be read in his pale eyes, in the hard smile on his meaty lips.

"I'll tell you what's happened," Pollock said. "You've cracked the whip for a long time. Now it's my turn to crack it. I'm damned if I'm gonna keep on covering up for you. When the Erdman girl ran off, she changed everything because she made a fool out of *me*, not you. That's why I had to send the boys after her, and it's why I lost Perkins."

The old days were gone, the good days when Seery could lead a double life and depend on Pollock to take care of the dirty chores that kept turning up. He gripped the saddle horn, looking down at the mountain of a man. Pollock's pride had been stung by what Betty Erdman had done. He had bragged too much in Bakeoven about having her. It wasn't grief over Perkins's death that had changed him; it was a case of injured vanity, and he was taking it out on Seery.

"We've got no cause to quarrel, Nate," Seery said, making his tone as friendly as he could. "We still need each other."

"The hell we do," Pollock snarled. "I've got my belly full of your fancy-Dan ways. Your granite bank building and your fine house won't do you no good with me. If you want my help on anything, you'll burn those notes. Savvy?"

"I've helped you as much as you've helped me," Seery said, anger rising in him at the man's blind obstinacy. "If it wasn't for me, there'd be a deputy in the valley right now. You'd better think that over before you break up our partnership."

He wheeled his chestnut and galloped out of the yard. Later he pulled the horse down to a walk. He needed time to think, and he had no reason to hurry. In one way he was trapped because he was certain his mother would kick him out of his job and his home if she knew about his life with Betty and his dealings with Pollock. Her good name was more important to her than her son.

But maybe it didn't make any difference.

He was sick of the sanctimonious life he lived in town. In trying to think of a simple way out of his predicament, he remembered that he had more than ten thousand dollars deposited in a bank in the county seat. He could take Betty out of the valley and marry her and use his money to get a start somewhere else. Marriage! Respectability! Why in hell did they mean so much to a woman?

The sun was down, and twilight had filled the valley with its thin uncertainty by the time he reached town. He offsaddled and watered and grained his chestnut, filled with a revulsion for the valley and its people. They thought he had all a man could ask for when in reality he had nothing. He had lived for years behind a false front of greatness, and now it had fallen in on him.

He went into the house through the back door, walking softly. He was hungry, but he didn't want his mother to know he was there. He heard voices from the parlor. Probably his mother and Lily. Lily! He made a sound of disgust.

He went into his study and shut the door. He lighted a lamp, then heard his door open and swung around. Lily stood there, staring at him hungrily. He swore at her. "Get out."

She shrank back, shocked by his words and his tone. She whispered, "What have you done to Daddy?"

"Nothing. Get out."

"Not until I know what's going on." She tipped her head back, filled with defiance that was totally unlike her. "Daddy almost rode a horse to death getting to town. He took another horse and started for the county seat. He said he was going after a deputy's badge for that fellow Sullivan who was here last night. Why, Matt?"

Seery sat down at his desk, suddenly tired. It was beyond his comprehension. The last thing he wanted was a deputy in the valley. Pollock? He laughed as he thought of what a deputy might mean. Nate Pollock would find out how much he needed Matt Seery.

"I guess Sullivan will make a good deputy, but I don't know any more than you do about what's going on." He motioned to the door. "Go on, now. Leave me alone."

When she didn't move, he got up and pushed her into the hall and closed and locked the door. He heard her call, "Mother Seery, Mother Seery."

A moment later his mother pounded on the door, her voice ominous as she said, "Open the door, Matthew." But he said nothing, and presently they went away.

He took his pipe out of his pocket and filled it, then threw his coat over a chair. As

179

he slipped on his smoking jacket, he stared at his father's picture. A hard man, Alexander Seery. Twelve years without him had not softened the memory. He remembered his father whipping him because he had once refused to fight, and his mother taking his part and the quarrel that had followed.

Now — and he had never been quite so honest with himself — he realized that it was his father who had shaped his life, turning him to Pollock, to Betty Erdman, who had given him the shape, if not the substance, of love. It had been his father's influence that had driven him to seek compensation for what had been lacking in the straitjacket his mother had forced upon him.

He swore, telling himself he would marry Betty right there in town, for everyone to see. That would hurt his mother more than anything else he could do, but he didn't care. He wasn't fooled by the love she pretended to give him. She had never, as long as he could remember, thought about anyone but herself.

He began pacing the room, considering what he would do after he left the valley. Ten thousand wasn't much money. He could forge a deed to the Manders place that might temporarily fool Sullivan. He'd get the fifty thousand. No need to cut Pol-

180

lock in on the deal. Then he'd ride out with Betty, and he'd have enough to live on.

He shook his fist at his father's picture, suddenly filled with crazy fury. "You God-damned old pirate," Seery shouted. "I'll make a piker out of you, a tinhorn piker."

He sat down at his desk, turning his thoughts to Sullivan. There was an ironic justice in the idea of Sullivan pinning on a star and going after Pollock. But Seery felt no real concern either way. He couldn't wait. He had no doubt about what would happen if he succeeded in swindling Sullivan. He'd have to kill him. It would take finesse, but it could be done with little real danger to a man with Matt Seery's reputation.

CHAPTER THIRTEEN

By the time Jim reached town after being fired at by Pollock's crew, he had made up his mind that Troy must be told what had happened. He shouldn't have any trouble finding her camp. She would not be more than a few miles east of the river.

He had supper in the hotel dining room, then went to Darket's livery stable, and rented a horse. His roan needed rest, and there was no way of foreseeing what would happen tomorrow. It was dark when he left town, riding west and then swinging south and finally east, completing a wide half-circle by the time he reached the end of the bridge, a precaution he took on the off chance that he was being watched.

Crossing the bridge, he rode east, thinking about what he would say to Troy. He had no illusions about her. The chances were he was wasting his time. She was almost home now; she would be anticipating the pleasure that would come from bringing Matt Seery to his knees.

He had no respect for either Pollock or Seery; for them he had no kindly feeling of any kind, but he did for Troy, and she was wrong. He had told her that on the sandy beach of the Dolores, and he'd tell her again. That was all he could do. He would fail, but he felt compelled to try.

The reason was not hard to find. He loved her, and perhaps it was a startling admission for him to make to himself. He had been avoiding it for months, telling himself he was curious about why she was the kind of woman she was. Perhaps he should have told her, but it would probably not have made any difference to her. Maybe it wouldn't now.

He had not thought she possessed any capacity for loving a man until two nights ago. He still couldn't be sure. Many a man had been fooled by a woman's kiss. Perhaps she had briefly permitted her innate feminine nature to come to the surface, making an unspoken promise because she needed him.

The thought troubled him, and when at last he reached her camp he was not sure of anything except the conviction he had started with. He had to try to make her see that the purpose which had brought her back to Rampart Valley was wrong.

The camp was close to the base of the south wall, the low-burning campfire a pinpoint of light in the darkness. The herd was bedded down along the creek to the north. All the men except the nighthawks were asleep, but as Jim dismounted he saw that Troy was still up, sitting beside the fire, her arms hugging her strong thighs as she stared at the flames. If she heard him ride up, she paid no attention, probably thinking it was one of the nighthawks riding in.

He called, "Troy."

She jumped up and swung toward him, crying, "Jim." She ran to him, and as she made the turn from the fire he saw that she was wearing a riding skirt. It was the first time that he had seen her when she wasn't wearing a pair of men's pants.

She came to him, asking anxiously, "Anything wrong, Jim?"

"Enough, but that isn't what brought me. I wanted to talk to you."

He sensed that she didn't approve of his coming, but she didn't scold him. She said only, her voice sharp, "Why take this risk if you didn't have to?"

"No risk," he said. "I wasn't followed. Nobody in the valley will know I'm hooked up with you."

"All right," she said. "Talk."

The command was typical of her, pointedly direct, with no hint of the roundabout approach that most women would have taken. "I'm in no hurry," he said, and taking her arm, swung her toward the cliff that was a black, scowling barrier below the star-lighted sky. "I've got considerable to say."

She was docile enough, letting him lead her to the jumbled pile of boulders at the base of the cliff. She sat down and waited, her knees pulled up under her chin, her arms around her thighs in much the same position she had assumed while sitting beside the fire.

The light was too thin to make out the expression on her face, but he felt her cool detachment. He decided he had no right to expect anything else. This was the Troy Manders he had known and puzzled over; it was not the Troy Manders who had briefly permitted herself the luxury of being a woman while they had been alone by the river.

"What the hell were you trying to do to me the other night?" he burst out.

"I could ask the same question. What were you trying to do to me?"

He sat down beside her. So he had

fumbled it the other night. After all these years of being self-sufficient, she had sincerely wanted to feel a man's strength and dominance. But how could he have known?

"Let it go," he said. "I came to tell you what's been going on."

He told her everything except the threat Gabe Dykens had made, and when he was done she asked, "Why did you butt into the Jarvis boy's trouble?"

Angry at her for asking a question that should never have been asked, he simply shrugged and sat silent.

"You should have stayed out of the Jarvis business," she said. "You have a fault I didn't know you had. I guess I didn't know there were any men left in the world like you."

"What are you talking about?"

"When I was a girl, I read about knights and chivalry and all that. My dad had a lot of history books. Poetry, too. It was natural enough, I guess, that I'd dream of knights in shining armor who defended the weak. That's what you think you are, but you're just being stupid. It's a dirty, stinking world, Jim, and you can't change it."

"I'm not going to try to change it, but the world's not as dirty and stinking as you think. You've been mired down in the mud

186

so long, hating Seery and Pollock, that you can't smell anything but the stink."

It was what he had come there to say. He hit her with the words, brutally, wanting only to make her see that there was another way of looking at life if she would open her eyes. But he could not tell if he had made any impression on her at all. She said lightly, "You sound as if you'd got religion."

"I didn't get it from you. Or Seery or Pollock. I guess young Jarvis getting plugged caught up with me. Or maybe it was talking to Jess Darket and having him tell me what your neighbors thought of your dad. Anyhow, I told you before you were wrong, and I'm saying it again."

She was silent. He could not tell if he had made her angry; he could not even tell what she was thinking. He waited, expecting an explosion, but it failed to come. Presently, her voice quite low, she said: "I remember Darket. And his little girl, who was just a child when I left. I remember the Erdmans, too. A shiftless lot with a greasy sack spread on the river. It's my guess she'd had a better life than she deserved."

He swore. "You're the stupid one, Troy. She's not much good, but —"

"Don't cuss me, Mr. Sullivan," she flared, "Or I'll use some brand-new words you never —"

"All right, all right. You said I sounded as if I had religion. Maybe I have, but I've had it a long time. I was hunting for something when I left home, and I've been hunting for it ever since. I've stayed with you for one year, two months —"

"To figure out what was the matter with me," she cried. "Well, maybe you found out or maybe you didn't, but one thing's sure. I won't make a fool out of myself again when I'm around you. Let's forget what happened the other night."

She had been thinking about it ever since, he thought. He had missed the one chance he'd had to change her life and his. He said bitterly: "Maybe you can forget it, but I can't. I'm in love with you. I didn't know it before. Seems like it hit me all of a sudden. Maybe that's the way it works. All I know is that I love you enough to try to keep you from killing something in you that's fine and decent."

He heard her take a long breath, heard her whisper, "Jim, say that again. That you love me."

"I *do* love you. I guess you've been figuring me for the world's biggest sucker, and maybe I am, but so help me, I love you."

"The world's biggest — Oh, Jim, Jim!"

She jumped up and started running toward the campfire. He caught her before she'd gone ten feet and swung her around to face him. "I'm not done talking and you're not done listening." He put an arm around her, drawing her close, and lightly placed his other hand upon one of her breasts, feeling its round firmness under her blouse. "You said you'd done your best to prove the Creator wrong about making you a woman. You think He ever put rigging like this on a man?"

"They're for babies," she whispered. "I want them. Some day I'll have them, but they've got to wait —"

"You don't have babies until you've had a man. Troy, you'll never have babies if you go on making hate the biggest thing in your life. Or if you do, you won't want them." He stepped back, dropping his hands to his sides. "I've seen what hate does to people. It'll destroy you. Burn you out. You're not an animal. You're a human being with a choice to make."

She didn't move for a long moment. He looked at her upturned face, a vague blur in the darkness, and he sensed the torment that was in her.

"It's easy for you to talk," she said finally. "I was there when my father died. I held his

189

head in my lap. I can't change now, Jim."

"You can change. It's all right to fight the things that are wrong, and Pollock and Seery are wrong. We'll fight them, but in the long run the important thing is what you're trying to do. If revenge is all of it, then I say it'll destroy you and me and maybe a lot of other people, too."

"You want me to turn around and go back to No Man's Land. That it, Jim?"

"Of course not. Drive into Bakeoven in the morning like you figured on doing. Go on to your place. Watch out for Pollock. He may take a crack at you as soon as he finds out what's happening."

"Then what's all this talk —"

"You haven't heard me," he said bitterly. "I'll say it again. The important thing is what you're trying to do. Your dad wanted to build a dam and have everybody share the water. He wasn't trying to beat anybody out of anything or even make a lot of money. He just wanted to help his neighbors. Isn't that right?"

"Yes, that's right," she said slowly. "I had almost forgotten."

"You'll find Betty Erdman in your house. Why don't you give her a chance to be something different than what Seery has made her instead of saying she got what she deserved?"

"Man, man," Troy breathed, "you don't know what you're asking."

"I know, all right. Every tongue in the valley will wag. It'll take courage . . ."

"Whatever my faults are, Jim," she said, "being a coward isn't one of them."

"I know that," he said.

He put his arms around her and forced her to come to him. He kissed her, but her response was not the same as it had been two nights ago. There was no life in her. She submitted, and that was all. He swung away from her and strode to his horse. When he mounted and rode away, he knew she was still standing there where he had left her.

He was hurt, and he had a terrible, numbing feeling that he had failed. Then again he wasn't sure. She couldn't change in a minute. It would take time. He had no doubt about his feelings. What he wanted was right here. He wasn't the answer to Troy's girlhood dreams. He was just a man wanting to make a home with a woman he loved, a home that would last.

CHAPTER FOURTEEN

Jim slept longer than he intended to the following morning, and even after he awoke he lay there exhausted. It had been late when he'd stabled the livery horse and stumbled up the hotel stairs to his room, but it wasn't lack of sleep that had worn him out. It was the uncertainty, the bitter knowledge that he still was not sure what Troy would do, or what she was thinking and feeling.

He stared at the torn wallpaper that hung from the ceiling in tattered ribbons. He rubbed his stubble-covered face, telling himself he ought to get a shave. Still he lay there, listening to a fly droning against the dirty window. On the wallpaper beside his bed hounds and riders were chasing their quarry against a flamboyant red background. Damned futile business, he told himself. Like him, they weren't getting anywhere. Then his eyes fastened on a heart which some lovesick cowboy had drawn. Inside the heart were the words, "Henry loves Sadie." Below it someone else had scrawled an obscene sentence about Henry and Sadie.

Jim turned his head, thinking about the love that had come to him. It was like being hit on the head. There was no sense to it. But maybe there was never any sense to being in love. He'd known men to do crazy things because they were in love, and he'd thought they were loco. Though a man could always find a woman, some sort of woman, now he knew how it was. Just any woman wouldn't do. Well, he'd been in love with Troy for a long time, even though he hadn't even been aware of his feeling. Now he knew why he had stayed on the job.

He sat up on the edge of the bed and rubbed his face again. Hell, she'd been with men for nine years, depriving herself of love because of her crazy obsession for revenge. He remembered that she had made him repeat that he loved her. By wanting to hear the words again, Troy had proved she was all woman. And like a fool, he'd said she was figuring him for the world's biggest sucker. After that, nothing had been right.

He got up and dressed. He poured water from the gaudy, hand-painted pitcher into the white bowl and washed. This business of sucking Seery into the irrigation project seemed foolish, but he'd go along with Troy because she expected it. After that? He just didn't know.

Buckling his gun belt around him, it occurred to him that Troy had depended on her own strength so long she would never admit she needed help beyond what any man she hired could give her. But she was bucking a stacked deck. He couldn't walk out on her now. He never would.

He had breakfast in the hotel dining room and walked to the bank. The weather had changed. Ugly clouds obscured the triple peaks of Telescope Mountain. There was no wind; the air was heavy and damp.

Jim found Seery at his desk. When the banker saw Jim come in, he rose, calling, "Good morning, Sullivan," and motioned for him to come through the gate at the end of the counter.

The banty with the nutcracker face glared at Jim. He said harshly: "This man came in yesterday asking for you. He was rude. He should —"

"Shut up," Seery snapped. As Jim came to his desk, he said apologetically: "You'll have to overlook that, Sullivan. He expects too much of some people and not enough of others."

"I shall inform your mother —" the teller began.

Seery wheeled and slapped him across the face. "You inform my mother of too many things, Vance." He turned to Jim. "We'll go into my private office to talk."

Jim, following Seery into the back room, saw the bright glitter of hate in the nutcracker's eyes as he stared at Seery's back. It was part of the pattern, Jim thought. The banty was Mrs. Seery's man, placed there to watch her son.

Jim dropped into a chair as Seery closed the door, thinking that Troy's coming would split the deal wide open. Seery moved past Jim and sat down behind his desk. For some reason he was uneasy, his face paler than usual. His hair was disheveled, and he looked as if he'd slept in his clothes.

"Before we start talking," Seery said, "keep in mind that I saved your life yesterday. I expect some return for a favor like that."

Jim rolled a smoke, not sure of what Seery had in mind. He said: "I know a lot of things about you, Seery — more than anyone else in Bakeoven. I'm giving you good return for your favor by keeping my mouth shut."

The banker drew his meerschaum from his pocket, filled it, and lighted it. "That's one way to look at it, but don't discount one fact. The Seerys have run this valley from the day my father came here. You can't blackmail me into anything, if that's what's in your mind. Don't try."

"You're bragging." Shrugging, Jim fished a match out of his vest pocket. "But I didn't come in here to have a ruckus with you. Besides, it isn't important."

"What is?"

"I offered you a proposition."

"And I've been thinking about it." Seery leaned back in his swivel chair, his long white fingers clutching its arms. "I told you my mother owns the bank. Vance Frane is a tattler. It must be obvious that we can't work along the lines you suggested."

"Maybe you've got another line to suggest."

"I have," Seery said. "I lied about the Manders girl owning her father's place. I had my reasons, which I won't go into. The property belongs to me, and I'll sell for the fifty thousand you offered. The bank, of course, will have no part of your operation."

Jim canted his chair back against the wall, holding his face rigid against the shock of Seery's words. It seemed incredible that he would lie so blandly. Was it possible that Troy had lied? Had she sold her father's ranch, and then, regretting it, decided to retake it by force? He dismissed the thought, knowing that he was being unfair to her.

"As I outlined my proposition," Jim said carefully, "the cooperation of the bank was part of the deal."

"It's impossible. My mother is an honest woman, Sullivan, not because she has any great sense of integrity, but because it pleases her vanity to have people believe in her."

Jim thought: You son of a bitch. Troy had you pegged right.

"If you want the property," Seery went on, "you'll have to put up the money in cash. How long will it take you to get it?"

A fist hammered on the door. Irritated by the interruption, Seery rose and opened the door. Vance Frane said, "There's a woman out here who insists on seeing you."

"I'm busy —"

"Not too busy to see me." Troy shoved Frane aside and motioned with her gun. "Back up, Seery."

Seery retreated, asking in a reedy voice, "Is this a hold-up?"

Troy came in and slammed the door shut. "No." She saw Jim and frowned. "So you beat me here."

She was wearing a brown blouse and a dark green riding skirt; her Stetson dangled down her back from the chin strap; and her gun belt was buckled around her waist. Jim rose, uncomprehending. She had intended to make a show, to drive her herd down Bakeoven's Main Street, and proclaim her defiance of Matt Seery openly. But something had changed her mind.

Jim said: "Looks like I did for a fact, ma'am. A funny thing just happened. Seery says he owns your place, but when I talked to you, you claimed you still had it. Who's lying?"

"He is, but it doesn't make any difference," Troy said. "The Triangle M is not for sale." She nodded at Seery. "Remember me?"

He had backed across the room and stood with his shoulder blades pressed against the opposite wall, his eyes on the gun in Troy's hand. He had not recognized her, Jim thought, and that was natural enough. She had been a slip of a girl when she'd left, and nine years had made their change in her. Then, suddenly, recognition came to Seery.

"You're Troy Manders," Seery said hoarsely. "You should have stayed away."

Troy shook her head, eyes still pinned on Seery's face. "When I left, I planned to come back. You and Pollock murdered my father. You were there with Pollock's bunch, but I know what the law is in this valley when it concerns the Seerys. That's why I came in to let you know I'm back. I won't look to the law to punish you. I'll do it myself."

Jim, watching Seery, realized that while he might be weak in opposing his mother, he had his share of courage. He had been startled by Troy's forcing her way into his room with a gun in her hand, but he straightened now, eyeing her, and he was not afraid.

"You're moving back on your ranch," Seery said. "That it?"

"That's it. My boys are driving a herd up the valley now. I have a good crew, Seery, good enough to take care of you and Pollock."

"Your accusation that I helped murder your father is too stupid to deny," Seery said, "but now I understand something that has been puzzling me. My beef herd had been gathered on Starlight Mesa, and it would have been driven into the valley today if someone hadn't stolen it and murdered my men. That would be some of your

199

bunch. Sullivan here tells me you had a ranch in No Man's Land. We all know that's an outlaw hangout. It seems a fair guess that you brought a wolf pack with you."

Troy was jolted, and she showed it. She leaned against the door, breathing hard, her gun at her side. To Jim it was no surprise. The Dykens boys might have had a fight with Seery's crew, or Gabe might have disregarded Troy's orders and had them dry gulched. Or Moloch might have done it himself. In any case, it bore out what Jim had told her. She could not keep the Dykens boys on her pay roll if she stayed in Rampart Valley.

"I might have sent someone here to kill you or Pollock," Troy said, "but I wouldn't have your men killed. This is a warning, Seery. Stay off the Triangle M."

She holstered her gun, opened the door, and stalked out. Seery crossed the room and closed the door. He turned back to Jim, giving him a tight grin. "You knew all the time she was coming back. You were running some kind of a sandy on me. You're a crook, Sullivan."

Jim tossed his cigarette stub lightly to the floor. "That's the funniest thing I ever heard, one crook calling another man a crook."

Seery sat down behind his desk. "I don't savvy your game."

"I don't savvy yours, either, claiming you owned the Manders property."

"It was quite simple. I need money. I planned to forge a deed. I had no idea how smart you were about things like that, but I thought I could fool you long enough to get my hands on your fifty thousand."

"Well, you're being honest, and that's something new. I figure you're not very smart, Seery, working all the angles you do."

"I'm smart enough," Seery said, "and I'll go on being honest with you. I suppose I'm a paradox, which should not be hard for you to understand. I've had to live under my father's shadow, and at the same time I was controlled by my mother, so I found pleasure in living two different lives."

"I'll be moseying," Jim said. "We won't do any business."

"On the contrary, we can do a good deal of business. You want the Manders place. I need money. It isn't important why except that I lost my beef herd. I can handle Pollock. How much would it be worth to you to have him wipe out the Manders girl's outfit?"

He said it casually, without feeling. Jim had no doubt now about his part in killing

Troy's father. Matt Seery was proposing mass murder, proposing it as cold-bloodedly as a man could.

Jim moved to the desk and looked down at Seery's pale face, the man's cold eyes meeting his. Jim said, "I've met some ugly bastards in my day, Seery, but you take top money."

The banker did not take offense. "In my opinion, you run me a close second. Now let's get down to cases. If you aren't serious about getting the Manders property, say so. If you are, I'll get it for you if you want it enough to pay me for my trouble. By the time Pollock gets done with the Manders girl, she'll be glad to sign the place over."

Jim's mouth tightened as he fought his temper. He could walk out and let it stand, or he could have the satisfaction of beating Seery half to death. Then another idea struck him. If he told Seery the truth, he might force the whole thing to a quick showdown.

"I lied," Jim said. "I'm working for Troy Manders. She had an idea you'd believe me and buy the place from her so you could sell it to me for a sizable profit, but I don't reckon you'd go at it that way. Maybe you don't know it, but Jess Darket has gone to the county seat to get a deputy's badge for me. When I get it, the first thing I'll do is to arrest you for the murder of Troy's father."

Seery listened, his face showing no surprise at what Jim said. His hands had been hidden by the desk. Now he jumped up, a gun gripped in his right hand, but he had no chance to fire. Jim had expected the move. He dived over the desk, getting hold of Seery's right wrist, and they spilled back across the swivel chair and went down in a tangle of arms and legs.

Seery got in one good blow to Jim's belly, then they rolled over, with Jim on top, and he grabbed Seery by both shoulders and beat his head against the floor. Seery held onto the gun. He cried out in pain, swearing and sobbing like a boy: he got his wrist free and rammed the gun against Jim's side, but he had been hurt and he had trouble easing the hammer back.

Jim rolled sideways, the gun under him, but it was flat against the floor, under his body, and Seery could not use it. He hit Seery in the face. He got up, and Seery, free now, brought the gun up, getting the hammer back at last. Jim kicked his arm. The gun went off, the bullet slicing into the wall. Stooping, Jim twisted the gun out of his hand and stepped back.

"If I didn't want to live in this valley," Jim

said, "I'd kill you now, but I'll wait for the star."

Blood drooled from the corner of Seery's battered mouth. He wiped it away, his eyes wild with the lust to kill that gripped him. He cried: "You'll never touch me. You'll never get that star, either."

"I'll get it," Jim said, and swung toward the door, where Vance Frane stood, his mouth open. "Mrs. Seery doesn't know it, but she's got a thieving, lying bastard for a son. You'd better tell her."

He walked past Frane, who began to scream for help. Jim turned on him, and said, "Shut up." Frane subsided, his face resembling a nutcracker more than ever.

Jim walked out of the bank, got his roan, and left town, riding south because he didn't want to catch up with Troy. He needed time to think. The play was in the open. Seery would do something. Probably run to Pollock. But not until it was dark.

He thought about the deputy's star, wondering if Seery could keep him from getting it. What would Darket do? He'd believe Seery. But suppose he didn't. If Jim arrested Seery, he'd probably find himself fighting everybody in the valley. Troy didn't want that. Neither did he.

If the valley people's trust in Seery could

be destroyed . . . Then Jim thought of Mrs. Seery. She probably wouldn't believe Jim if he went to her, but it was worth a try. At least she'd have something to think about. She might already have her suspicions, and she would begin to add things up. If Jim judged her right, she'd sacrifice Matt to save her good name. He swung his roan back to town.

CHAPTER FIFTEEN

Troy was too dazed to think straight when she walked out of the bank. The news that the Dykens boys had disobeyed her orders and murdered Seery's men had hit her harder than anything had hit her since the murder of her father. Mounting, she left town on the run, suddenly obsessed with a frantic desire to see her old home.

After talking to Jim last night, she had given up the idea of driving her herd down Bakeoven's Main Street. It had been a childish plan, anyhow. Someone might get hurt, and she'd turn folks against her before she had a chance to tell them why she was back and what she wanted to do. So she had ordered Baldy Cronin to swing the cattle around Bakeoven and push them hard so they'd reach the Triangle M before dark.

She had come on, deciding to tell Seery she was here, confident that he would run to Pollock and that the thing would come to a head at once. If there had to be a fight, it might as well come now. She was within her right, and she had no doubt that her crew would win.

Now, with the town behind her, she slowed up, looking ahead at Telescope Mountain, most of it hidden by the clouds, at the trough of the valley that lay between the tall sandstone walls, at the line of willows along the creek and the scattered ranches, so familiar she might have been gone a week instead of nine years. Bailey. Matson. Yates. She remembered their names; she remembered the faces that went with the names; and more important than either, she remembered what her father had said.

"The only way this valley can be prosperous over a period of time is to put in an irrigation system," he had said repeatedly. "I've seen Rampart Creek so low after a dry season that it didn't run enough water for the stock. We should work together and make a community enterprise out of it."

That, of course, was the last thing Pollock had wanted. With an adequate water supply, more ranchers would settle in the valley, and Pollock would have to share his summer grass on Telescope Mountain. That meant more people to watch what went on in Nate's end of the valley, probably more law and order, greater strength to oppose Pollock.

During the nine years she had been gone, she had kept her thoughts so completely on revenge that she had forgotten what her father was like, what he believed in, what he had wanted to do. Now that she was back in the valley, her father's precepts were in her mind again, and she was ashamed that she had not kept them before her all the time.

The strangest part of it was that Jim Sullivan, in the short time he had been in the valley, shared something of her father's thought. What hurt her was the knowledge that Jim was right and she was wrong. What was even stranger, in her eyes, was that she was in love with him. She had known it for a long time, but she had refused to admit it because she had not wanted anything to divert her from the grim purpose that had guided her for so long.

Then, that night along the Dolores, something had happened to her. Because she had been frightened by the possibility that she was sending Jim to his death, she had kissed him, on a sudden, wanton impulse, and from that moment she had been fiercely aware of the knowledge that the Lord had known what He was doing in making her a woman.

Then, last night, Jim had told her that he loved her but that he thought she was using him, making a sucker of him. It had been too much. He had kissed her, but the spark was gone. After he left, she knew why. He had been right. Loving him had not kept her from trying to use him, and that made her a sorry kind of woman.

The long sleepless night had humbled her. Before morning came, her decision was made. She would not let her pride stand between her and Jim; she would get down on her knees to him if she had to. For the time being, at least, she would forget her passion for revenge. Somehow she would find a way to convince him she loved him.

But she couldn't now. Jim had been right about the Dykens boys. If she hadn't been controlled by her burning desire for revenge, she would have let them go before she left the Cimarron. She should have foreseen what they'd do. They were the only men in her crew she disliked. She had been a little afraid of them, of Gabe, anyway, for she had sensed what was in his mind. More than that, she should have foreseen what would happen when she sent them to Starlight Mesa to scatter Seery's beef herd.

Now, in this bitter hour of self-condemnation, the burden of guilt was too much to bear. Because of her, men had died, men who had never hurt her, cowhands who happened to be working for Matt Seery.

The sun was noon high when she reached the Triangle M. Dismounting, she tied at the hitch rail, sick with the dull ache of regret. But nothing could undo what had been done, and wishing she hadn't sent the Dykens boys to Starlight Mesa was the most futile of wishes.

For a long time she stood motionless, a weird feeling possessing her that she had lost all sense of time. The little house that her father had built was not changed at all, even to the row of red hollyhocks along the front. Mrs. Yates had given her the seeds, and she had planted them. She had kept the grass around the house cut. She had planted a small garden alongside the creek where her father had put in a low dam and had dug a ditch across the upper end of the garden. The barn. Tool shed. Corrals. So little difference.

She had supposed the place would be deserted, the windows knocked out, the yard overgrown with weeds. She stood there gripping the gnawed old hitch pole while time flowed by. She fought a desire to cry. She couldn't, not Troy Manders. Crying was for other women, ordinary women who wore ribbons in their hair and dresses with ruffles, and pinched their cheeks to make them glow with color when a man was taking them to a dance. To hell with that!

She drew her Winchester from the boot and went up the path to the front door, thinking about the unpleasant task that faced her. Betty Erdman was there: Betty Erdman who had kept the grass cut and watered the hollyhocks and planted the garden; Betty Erdman who belonged to Matt Seery.

Troy went in without knocking. She closed the door and leaned against it, fighting for breath. The lump in her throat threatened to choke her. Even the inside of the house was little different than it had been the night she had left nine years ago.

She remembered the day her father had finished the house and a wagon had come from Bakeoven with the furniture. She had been eleven, but she remembered because they had been living in a cabin with crude homemade furniture.

She'd stood in this room while her father and the freighter had brought the things from the wagon: the shiny leather couch, the red plush chair that to her had been the very acme of luxury, the oak table that had made the men grunt and pant, the book-case with the glass doors that had been handled as carefully as if it were a box of eggs. The books had been in the cabin. Her father had owned books as long as she could remember. She had helped her father place them on the shelves, taking great care because her father had said they held the learning of the world.

Even the rag rugs on the floor were the same. Everything was spotless, without a hint of dust. Betty Erdman was a good housekeeper, Troy thought, though perhaps it had never been in Betty's mind that what she did she did for Troy Manders. Still, Troy knew, she owed Betty a debt.

She wiped her hands across her face. She could not hold back the tears. Then she straightened and set her rifle against the wall. Betty Erdman was standing in the kitchen doorway staring at her, shocked and a little frightened.

She said, "I'm Troy Manders," ashamed that Betty had caught her crying.

She heard Betty gasp, and saw the pretty face go white as she said in a shocked tone: "Troy Manders! It isn't possible, after all this time."

Troy smiled. The weakness that homecoming had aroused in her had suddenly gone. There was something pathetic about Betty in her pink gingham dress that had been designed to show off her body to its best advantage. Her red-gold hair was braided and pinned on top of her head.

Seery's woman! In spite of herself, Troy could not help feeling a touch of envy as she thought of her own strong thighs and work-hardened muscles, her sun-blackened skin and her calloused hands. There was much she could learn from Betty Erdman.

"I'm Troy Manders, all right," she said. "I've come back to live here. My herd will be on Triangle M grass before dark."

"You can't," Betty cried. "Have you forgotten Nate Pollock?"

"I could never forget him," Troy said. "He murdered my father. That's why I came back."

"I — I guess I'm trespassing," Betty said. "Give me a few minutes to pack some things and I'll get out."

Troy crossed the room to the girl and took her hands. "You haven't any place to go, have you?"

"No, but —"

"You're staying here as long as you want to. Jim Sullivan told me what happened in town. He works for me."

Betty drew her hands away from Troy and turned toward the kitchen, a lonely and unhappy woman who knew how Troy would regard her. A hand came up to clutch her throat.

"I couldn't stay here, with you knowing what I've been," she said in a choked voice. "No other woman, I mean, decent woman, would understand why I'm what I am."

"I'm not a very decent woman," Troy said. "What I've done is more terrible than anything you've done, but we can't go back and live the last week over — not even the last hour; so the only comfort I can find is the hope I can make tomorrow better."

"But I can't," Betty said. "I killed Bob Jarvis, Miss Manders. I killed him just like I'd pulled the trigger myself."

"Then I'm three times worse than you are, because I killed Seery's men on Starlight Mesa; but I'm not going to spend the rest of my life blaming myself. I can't live that way. I'm going to seek forgiveness, and somewhere I'll find it." She stopped, realizing that Betty could not understand what she was trying to say, and realizing, too, that Betty was not taking Jarvis's death as lightly as Jim had thought. "Do you remember my father?"

"Of course. I remember everybody liked him. I've looked through his books. I've read his Bible, and I think I know him because I've studied the passages he underlined. He must have been a good man."

"A better man than I will ever be a woman," Troy said, her voice made bitter by the accusation of her memory. "If you knew him, you would understand you would be welcome here."

"But you'd be disgraced —"

"No," Troy said. "Or if I was, disgrace is one thing I'm not afraid of. I owe you a great debt for taking care of things. I want you to stay. Can't you believe that?"

She saw hope break across Betty's face, a pathetic eagerness to accept her invitation. She thought she understood the conflicting tides of emotion that were in the girl, her need for the friendship of what she would call a "decent woman."

"Matt wouldn't let me stay here," Betty whispered. "If you kept me here, he'd strike at you."

"I want him to," Troy said. "He's more to blame for my father's murder than Pollock was. As much, anyway."

Betty's hand was still at her throat. She said, "I don't understand."

"Don't worry about it," Troy said. "I just

want you to know that I'm not afraid of either Matt Seery or Nate Pollock. It seems to me the only question is whether you're in love with Seery."

"In love with him?" Betty cried. "I hate him. I planned to kill him last night, but I couldn't, and I couldn't let Jim Sullivan kill him, either. I don't know why. I just couldn't. But I don't want to go back to him. You've got to believe that."

"Then you'll stay," Troy said, as if it were settled. "I'll put my horse up. If you'll fix me something to eat . . ."

"Of course," Betty said eagerly. "I baked some cookies. I like to bake. I'd have gone crazy if I hadn't been able to cook."

Troy gave her a quick smile and left the house. After she had watered and fed her horse, she lingered in the back yard for a time, her eyes on the aspen-covered slope to the west, and listened to the liquid whisper of the creek, a song she had loved and almost forgotten. There had been no streams like it in the Neutral Strip.

She thought of the little park that would be filled with water if she built the dam, of the gold in the wagons. Only Longhorn Flannigan knew it was there, and he didn't know how much. It was more than enough to build a bunkhouse and make the other improvements that would be necessary, now that she was going to make a real spread out of the Triangle M. The trouble was, she would have no beef to market for a long time unless she bought some feeders from the valley ranchers. That would take a big chunk of her money. Or if she didn't do that, she still would need the money to go through the lean years that lay ahead. She couldn't afford to put much into the dam. Even if the valley ranchers helped, there would be supplies to buy, an engineer to hire, money she would be expected to spend.

She walked to the house, pondering. Funny how her thinking had changed in the last few days. The last few hours, for that matter. She had not really thought much about staying here when she had left the Cimarron. It hadn't seemed important. Now there was no doubt in her mind. This was her home, her kind of country. Nothing could drive her away again.

When she went into the house through the back door, she saw that Betty had set the table. It had been a long time since breakfast, and she suddenly realized she was hungry. She ate with a man's appetite. Betty filled her cup with coffee as soon as it was empty, saying, "There's more biscuits in the warming oven."

"This is plenty," Troy said. "It's nice to sit at a table again after being on the trail so long."

"I should have brought in some flowers," Betty said. "I guess I was afraid to go outside."

"You can stop being afraid," Troy said. "We're going to be good friends."

Betty took a long breath. "Miss Manders, I've been thinking. You're awfully kind, but you've forgotten how people talk in a country like this. You need neighbors, and you won't have them if I stay."

"If people don't like my friends, they won't like me," Troy said. "Now you quit your fretting."

Betty shook her head. She walked around the table to the door that led into the front room, restless and nervous and not knowing quite how to say what was in her mind. There was still a girlish immaturity about her, Troy thought, although she must be twenty or older. Her hair was quite dark against her light skin, so thick and long there seemed to be too much of it. She wasn't anything like what Troy had supposed she would be, and she wondered how Betty had got into the affair with Seery in the first place.

"When I go to town, which isn't often," Betty said, "people treat me as if I had smallpox. You don't know how it feels, and I don't want you to find out on my account."

"I don't care, Betty." Troy rose and walked to the girl. "I was looking at your dress. Did you make it?"

"I make all my clothes," Betty said. "I have to."

"You sew awfully well. I don't. I want you to help me. And I need help with my hair." Troy paused, finding that she could not tell Betty she had to change her life because she was in love with Jim. She blurted, "Damn it, I'm going to be a lady if it kills me."

Betty stared at her, shocked. "But I'm not a lady, Miss Manders."

Troy wasn't listening. She was looking past Betty through a window. Gabe Dykens and Moloch were in front of the house. Of all the times for this to happen . . . If Jim were here . . .

"I've got company," Troy said. "Stay in the kitchen. I'll handle this."

She walked across the front room, glancing back to see that Betty was not in sight. She opened the door just as Gabe stepped up on the porch. She said: "You're fired, Gabe. You knew what my orders were about

219

Seery's crew."

Gabe's face was longer and more wolfish than she had ever seen it. He said, "I ain't gonna be fired."

He pushed past her into the house. Troy said in a flat voice: "Ride out, Gabe. Take Molly. Get out of this country and stay away, or I'll see you hang for killing those men."

Gabe cuffed back his hat with a quick, upward thrust of his thumb. He said: "Let's talk sense. I've paid back anything I owed you for saving our necks that time, so we're square. If you start gabbing about Seery's crew, I'll see folks know why you're here and what you told us to do. You ain't in no shape to fire me, Troy."

"The hell I'm not," she flung at him. "I say you'll hang —"

"Not me. Molly done it before I could stop him. Last night he got into a ruckus with Enoch and killed him. Now there's just me and Molly, and all on account of you."

"I told you to see Molly behaved himself," she cried furiously. "Don't load his crimes onto me."

"No sense of us quarreling." He took a quick step to her and gripped her shoulders. "You need me and you know it. I like you —"

"I don't like you and I never have. I'm sorry I kept them from hanging you. Now will you —"

"You never fooled me about why you saved our necks. You just wanted to use us. All right, you have, and I ain't kicking, but I didn't know you were a bitch. After you and Sullivan —"

She hit him in the belly with her fist, a hard blow that jolted breath out of him. She tried to pull her gun, but he grabbed her arm and twisted it, shouting: "You're my woman. Sullivan ain't man enough for you and never was. I aim to show you I am."

Fear was not a familiar emotion to Troy. She had always been able to handle men, and none of them had ever laid a hand on her, but now she was afraid, and she knew her strength could not match his. He yanked her to him and held her face close to his; she caught the fetid odor of his breath, saw the glow of desire that was in his eyes, and she screamed.

He kissed her, smothering her scream. She couldn't breathe. His arms were around her, holding her so tightly she couldn't fight. She kicked him on the shin, but she might as well have kicked the wall.

He drew his mouth back, laughing at her. "Sullivan never kissed you like that, did he?

Hell, I'm more man than he ever thought of being. I'll do what you want done and you'll give me what I want, and that's a good deal for both of us."

He picked her up and started toward the bedroom. She kicked, she cursed him and beat at him with her fists. She screamed, "Jim'll kill you."

He laughed again. "You've got that wrong. I'm gonna kill him."

Gabe was a full step through the bedroom door when something hit him on the head, the sound a dry, snapping crack. He stumbled; his arms went slack and he dropped Troy. Mouthing obscene curses, he wheeled as Betty struck him again with a stick of stove wood. She had both hands on it; she hit him with all her strength, and he went down on his knees.

Troy was hurt by the fall, but she jumped up, gaining the moment she needed. Before Gabe got back on his feet, her gun was in her hand. She said in a low tone: "I ought to kill you. I will if you're not out of here in ten seconds."

He stood there, swaying, a trickle of blood running down his lean face and dripping from the point of his chin. He stared at Betty, too dazed to think straight. Troy said: "Unbuckle your gun belt. Then get out.

Don't ever let me see you again."

Mechanically he unbuckled the belt and let it drop. He staggered to the front door and opened it. He said thickly: "Before this is done you'll come crawling to me. You'll see."

He went out, still reeling, and got on his horse. Troy stood in the doorway breathing hard, weak with relief, and she didn't move until the Dykens brothers rode away. Maybe they'd keep going, she thought dully. If they didn't, she would have more trouble, and she had enough.

Betty said: "I'm sorry, Miss Manders. I had to go outside for a club. Nothing in the wood box but chips. That's why I was so slow."

Troy shut the door and sat down on the red plush chair. She wiped her mouth, but Gabe's kiss seemed ineradicable. She shivered, fear still in her. Finally she said, "I owe you more than I can ever repay."

"You don't owe me anything," Betty said. "Not anything."

Troy didn't move. The minutes fled by. Nine years of living among men, and nothing like this had happened until she returned to the valley. She bowed her head and shut her eyes, still trembling, and asked herself how wrong a woman could be.

Betty had moved to a window. Her fright-
ened voice jarred Troy back to reality:
"We've got more trouble, Miss Manders.
Pollock's coming."

CHAPTER SIXTEEN

Seery pulled himself into his chair after Jim left the bank. Taking a white handkerchief from his pocket, he began to dab at his mouth. He ached in a dozen places, but there was a sense of frustration in him that hurt far more than the beating Jim Sullivan had given him. It was the first time he had ever actually fought with a man, the first time he had ever tried to kill a man.

Vance Frane remained in the doorway, his toothless gums clamped so tightly that his chin swept upward toward his long nose. He said hoarsely, "I'll get some men and —"

"Go back to work," Seery said.

"But Matthew, your father would have —"

"God damn you, shut up," Seery shouted. "I'm not my father and I'm not my mother, and I'll take care of Sullivan in my own way. Go back to work or I'll fire you."

He couldn't, and he knew it, but the threat

was enough to make Frane scurry away. Seery kept dabbing at his mouth, and then, for some reason which he did not try to analyze, the feeling of frustration left him. He had always been repelled by the prospect of being involved in physical violence, although he enjoyed watching fights and there had been times when he had found pleasure in seeing men die.

He remembered exactly how it had been with Manders, the girl lying there, out cold. He had enjoyed that, perhaps in much the same way other men enjoyed going hunting and shooting a buck. As he recalled what had happened that night, he forgot the throbbing pain in his face.

The girl should have been killed, too. But no one could have foreseen she would come back, least of all turn into the kind of woman she was, and have a hardcase like Jim Sullivan working for her. Then it occurred to him that Betty was living in the Manders house and that Troy would find her there.

He swore and got up. He had to move fast or he'd lose Betty. A hell of a thing for a man to let his happiness be so bound up with a woman's, but that's the way it was; and he could not escape the horrifying fear that Betty was done with him, that she'd meant what she said, and that he'd delayed so long and broken so many promises he'd finally driven her away from him.

He tried to put the possibility out of his mind, telling himself that when she finally realized he was making good on his promises she would give herself to him as completely as she had when she had first discovered she loved him. He wadded up his bloody handkerchief and shoved it into his pocket as he stepped into the bank.

"Vance, go over and jack up that barber," Seery said. "We've been too easy on him. He's a year behind on his interest."

"Only six months, Matthew."

"Too long. Go over and tell him to pay up."

Frane started to object, for it had never been the bank's policy to push a man when he'd had bad luck. Both Frane and Seery knew Ed Maylor's wife had been sick and he'd sent her to Denver. But there was something hard and forbidding in Seery's face, and Frane left without a word.

The instant Frane was gone, Seery went to the safe and took out the folder that held Pollock's notes. He put them into his pocket and replaced the folder. The temptation was strong to help himself to the gold, but he had no illusions about what his mother would do.

The gold would be missed at once, and he'd have the law on his tail. On the other hand, it was improbable that Frane would discover the missing notes for a long time. When he did, Seery would deny he had taken them. It wouldn't make any difference anyhow. By that time he'd be a thousand miles from Rampart Valley.

He returned to his private office, took the empty shell out of his gun, and slipped a new load into place. He'd make a deal with Pollock or he'd kill him. He'd get out of the valley with Betty, and that would end his life here. He should have done it a long time ago, he thought, as he dropped the gun into his pocket.

Funny how a woman got hold of a man, especially when he discovered he was about to lose her. He had taken Betty for granted. He shouldn't have. There had been plenty of storm warnings. He knew she had grown weary of his broken promises, but he had never once thought she'd try to get away. She had wanted marriage and the position that would give her in a community. All right, she'd have it, somewhere a long way from Bakeoven. They'd cross Telescope Mountain into Utah, they'd get married in Moab, and then they'd go to California. It had been one of the promises he'd made, and now he'd fulfill it.

He went back into the bank to wait for Frane. The man was gone a long time, too long, and Seery became impatient. He was furious when he thought of Sullivan and the Manders girl and his murdered crew. But Pollock would take care of them. Anyhow, the important thing was to get away. He paced the room, his impatience growing with each dragging minute.

He walked to the front door and looked out. Frane was coming. Seery moved back to his desk. The instant Frane came in, Seery said: "I'm going home, Vance. That bastard hurt me more than I realized. I think I'll go to bed."

"I'll take care of things." Frane cleared his throat. "About Maylor, Matthew. He can't pay his interest now. You know how it's been. I told him I'd see if we wouldn't let it go for another three months."

Seery glared at him, pretending to be angry. "I told you . . ." Then he shrugged. "Never mind. I'll talk to you tomorrow."

He left the bank, satisfied that Frane had not suspected anything, but as he turned the corner and walked down the side street doubts began to plague him. Frane would run to his mother, and she'd raise hell about putting the pinch on Maylor.

Not that she gave a damn. It was just part of the way she lived, wanting folks to think she was a white-haired angel. Frane had never liked him. Nothing would please the old fool more than to catch him at something like taking Pollock's notes. But Frane wouldn't think of looking in that folder, Seery kept reassuring himself. Still the doubt lingered. He didn't want to cut his bridges behind him until he was actually on his way with Betty.

Seery circled his house, hoping his mother wouldn't see him. He didn't feel like talking to her or Lily Darket. He didn't want them to see his battered face and start asking questions. He had a hell of a time standing up to both of them when they started asking questions.

He reached the alley behind his house and went into the barn. Probably his mother was taking a nap. She usually did at this time of day. The chestnut whinnied, but for once Seery didn't take time to pet him. He saddled as quickly as he could, mounted, and rode down the alley.

As soon as he was out of town, he put his chestnut into a run. He'd have to get a horse from Pollock for Betty. That worried him, because Pollock was as ornery as hell about his horses. But he'd manage. The notes in his pocket gave him the upper hand.

A mile or so from town he saw Troy Manders' herd, moving at a snail's pace. He circled them, not wanting to talk to other men or be recognized. Any of a number of things might happen which would prevent his leaving today. Pollock might have gone up on the mountain to drive his beef herd down.

He swung back onto the county road, the need for haste throbbing in him like a pulse beat. He wondered briefly if Sullivan had gone to the Manders place. Well, it wouldn't make any difference if he had. Pollock and Bert Knoll would welcome the chance to nail him.

Then, for some obscure reason, he thought of how much his decision was costing him. He was leaving a ranch that was his, a job in the bank and in the freight-and-stage office. If he stayed, he would inherit all of it some day. But some day was too long to wait. He remembered his boasts the other night when he'd shaken his fist at his father's picture and said he'd make Alexander Seery look like a piker. If he did, it would be somewhere else. He didn't really care how much his running away cost him. He never again wanted to see his father's tough, forbidding face that hung on his study wall. He wanted to get away from his mother, from Vance Frane and Lily Darket and all the things and people he hated.

Getting away, getting away, getting away. The chestnut's hoofs hammered against the red dirt, keeping time with the rhythm of the words. He was glad things had shaped up the way they had, forcing him to do something he had wanted to do all the time. The trouble was, he'd been in a rut, lacking the will to break free.

He had not seen anything of Troy when he turned up the lane that led to Pollock's ranch. She had probably reached her place. It was just as well he hadn't overtaken her. He stepped down. Pollock was at the corrals with Ace Rush and young Tafoya. Knoll was probably in the house.

Pollock came toward him, a great laugh rolling out of him when he saw Seery's bruised face. He said, "Well now, Mr. Seery, did you meet up with a grizzly?"

"Sullivan," Seery said. "I was wrong. You're right. We've got to get him now."

Pollock slapped his leg and laughed again. "Ain't it funny how a man's notions change when he gets a banging around? Now you know how Bert feels."

"I know, all right," Seery said. "You're going to know, too. Sullivan is working for Troy Manders. She's back in the valley with a herd she figures on throwing on her dad's old range. She's here to square up for beefing her old man."

Pollock blinked, his moon-like face going cold. He said harshly, "You're lying."

"I've never lied to you in my life, Nate. She came into the bank and told me why she was here. I passed her herd on my way out here. Go look for yourself."

"I will." Pollock wheeled and motioned to his men. "Saddle up." He turned back to Seery. "If you're telling the truth, we'll run her critters back across the Dolores."

"There's a better way, Nate."

Pollock's jaws were hard-set, muscles at their hinges bulging out like twin marbles. "Still calling the dance tune, Mr. Seery?"

"I've got a deal," Seery said. "It's a good deal for you. The only reason I'm offering it is because I want Betty. You going to listen, or not?"

Pollock jerked his big head at the men. "Hustle up, Rafe. Ace, you go into the house and get Bert. He ain't hurt so bad he can't ride." Again he swung to face Seery, his feet planted apart in the red dust, his head bent so that his chins bulged out in a great roll of fat. His attitude plainly showed that he was skeptical of any deal Seery had to offer, but he said, "I'll listen."

"The Manders girl is in her house with Betty," Seery said. "Sullivan may be there, too. Kill him. I don't care what happens to the Manders girl. All I want is Betty. Fetch her here and I'll swap your notes for her. I have them in my pocket."

"I'll take them now," Pollock said.

"You'll get them when you deliver Betty, not before." Seery's right hand was in his pocket. "Don't push me, Nate, or I'll kill you."

The big man rocked back and forth on his heels, pale eyes half closed. Tafoya was saddling the horses. Rush and Knoll were leaving the house. When Pollock showed no inclination to either accept or reject the offer, Seery said sharply: "Don't figure me wrong, Nate. I'm leaving the valley and I'm taking Betty. I want a gentle horse for her to ride. It's a good deal for you, twenty thousand in exchange for a woman."

"So," Pollock murmured. "You're plumb salty all of a sudden."

Never in his life had Seery felt as he did now. He wasn't afraid. This had to work or nothing ever would. More than Betty was at stake. He had to believe in himself. If Alexander Seery was watching from whatever hell he had gone to, he'd see some of his tough strength in his son.

Seery laughed, a strange sound that wasn't entirely a laugh, a matter of defiance as much as anything, to match Pollock's go-to-hell laugh that always rolled up out of him when he was in a tight spot. But there was a sort of humor in this situation if a man was sure enough of himself to see it. Seery had broken away from his past today. Now, more than anything else, more even than wanting Betty, he was driven by a wild desire to measure up to the tough standard Alexander Seery had set.

"Maybe not so sudden," Seery said. "Do I look soft, Nate?"

He had moved back so that he could watch the men coming from the house and still keep the gun he held in his pocket on Pollock. He wasn't quite sure of the expression on the fat man's face, but he thought it was astonishment as much as anything, and Pollock's mild words, "No, Mr. Seery, you don't look soft," satisfied him.

"All right, go get Betty," Seery said. "The old days are gone, Nate, but you don't care about that. You figured you don't need me any more."

"No, I don't care," Pollock murmured. "So long, Mr. Seery. It's been fine, real fine, me doing the dirty work and you sitting in the bank with your feet cocked on your desk and eating mighty high on the hog." He wheeled, calling, "Let's ride, boys."

Seery watched them leave, asking himself what Pollock meant. Then he thought he knew, and he cursed Nate Pollock with every word he could think of. They intended keeping Betty, and he wondered in a wild surge of jealousy what had gone on between her and Pollock all this time. Maybe she had tried to run away from Pollock, not him, and she had been afraid to tell him.

Now, certain that he had guessed right, he began to sweat. He shouldn't have come here. It would have been better if he had gone directly to Manders' house. He would have to kill Pollock when he returned. It was the only way he would ever get Betty.

CHAPTER SEVENTEEN

Jim was scared as he tied his horse in front of the Seery house and went up the walk to the front porch. It was an odd sort of fear. He had never felt anything like it before. Perhaps everyone who knew Mrs. Seery was afraid of her. Even Matt.

Now that Jim saw the Seery place in daylight, he realized it was grander than he had thought. A picket fence surrounded the big lawn; the row of cottonwoods that ran along the street side of the yard threw a patch of shade against the sunlight that momentarily covered most of the grass.

The house was as out of place in Bake-oven as a second thumb on a man's hand. It had two stories, with more room than the Seerys would have needed if they'd had ten children instead of one. The gingerbread architecture was more typical of a mining camp than a cow town, with its jigsaw cornices and tiny fence on the very top of the building.

Jim crossed the porch and jerked the bell pull, a little ashamed of himself because he could not overcome the fear that the prospect of talking to Mrs. Seery aroused in him. Real danger, such as he faced in the street when he had shot Perkins, had never bothered him, but the thought of facing Mrs. Seery and saying what he was determined to say brought icy fingers out of nowhere to clutch and twist his insides.

The door opened a crack, and Lily Darket peeped through the slit. She said, *"You,"* as if he were a crawling thing, and would have shut the door if he hadn't put his foot against it.

"Funny thing about this house," Jim said. "If I hadn't shoved my foot against the door the other night, I wouldn't have got in to see Matt."

"What do you want?" the girl asked, her tone frosty.

Jim decided he didn't like her, even if she was Jess Darket's daughter. He could see how Matt Seery had got himself trapped, engaged to Lily when he probably loved Betty Erdman with as much passion as he was capable of feeling for anyone.

"I want to see Mrs. Seery," Jim said.

"She's busy."

"You'd better let me in," Jim said, exasperated, "or I'll jam this door open and run over you like a stampeding mossyhorn."

Reluctantly the girl opened the door. "I hate you, Mr. Sullivan. Why my father thinks you'd make a good deputy . . ."

"You know about that?"

"I know, all right. I know he'll ride a horse to death getting to Placerville and he'll kill another horse getting back. And for what? Just to give a star to a man we don't know anything about —"

"Tell Mrs. Seery I'm here," Jim interrupted.

Lily turned, her long, dark skirt swirling around thick ankles. She opened the door into the living room, went in, and closed it behind her. A strange daughter for a man like Jess Darket, Jim thought, a girl driven by her frantic desire to become part of the Seery family. Alongside Betty Erdman she wasn't much, but according to Bakeoven's standards she was good and Betty was bad.

Lily returned, leaving the door open into the living room. "Mrs. Seery will see you," she said curtly.

Jim walked past her into the big living room, his hat in his hand. Mrs. Seery stood by a heavy mahogany table, a claw-like hand upon it. She was still wearing the black silk dress with the tight lace collar, her face as frosty as a chill winter morning.

"I am surprised you'd have the temerity to come here again," Mrs. Seery said.

Jim took a deep breath, fighting the crazy desire to run that crowded him. He glanced around the room, finding it much as he supposed it would be: a maroon carpet on the floor, curtains at the windows, massive furniture with black leather adding a tone of luxury to the chairs and couch, wallpaper with small boats sailing across a sullen sea, and a great picture of Alexander Seery in an ornate frame hanging above the fireplace. The elder Seery must have had a great weakness for being photographed, for it was the third picture Jim had seen of him.

Jim brought his eyes to Mrs. Seery. "I don't care for this chore any more than you do, ma'am." He motioned to Lily Darket, who stood glowering in the doorway behind him. "What I have to say is not for her ears."

"I won't leave Mrs. Seery alone with you," Lily cried.

"It's all right, dear," Mrs. Seery said. "Step outside."

Her manner clearly indicated she was confident she could handle any saddle tramp who forced his way into her house, and her lips were a thin, forbidding line across her face. Jim waited until the door closed, still fighting a desire to run.

"Troy Manders is in the valley," Jim said. "I work for her. She's moving back onto her ranch and she's bringing a herd to stock her range."

"Well?"

"When she left," Jim hurried on, "she promised herself she would come back and punish the men who killed her father."

"They were outlaws who left the country a long time ago," Mrs. Seery said harshly. "We have had many men like them, men like you. They never stay here."

"Nate Pollock and his crew killed her father," Jim said. "Your son was among them."

She might have been frozen there. Her expression did not change except that it became more exaggerated, the lips more tightly pressed, and her eyes narrowed until they were nearly closed. She breathed, "You've said enough, Mr. Sullivan. Good day."

"I'm not done. I'm guessing your position in this community and the Seery name mean more to you than anything else, but you'll lose both if the truth comes out. Your son has been living with Betty Erdman in the Manders house."

She swayed, her hand clutching the edge of the table, no longer able to hide her feelings. She was hit hard by what he had said, but Jim had the passing thought that she had suspected it all the time and had not been too much concerned so long as it wasn't known.

"If I were a man, I'd kill you," she whispered. "What have you to gain, telling me this?"

"Nothing for me, but maybe something for Troy. She could do this valley a lot of good, but not as long as Pollock and your son are in cahoots, and as long as the valley people think Matt is sitting at the right hand of God."

"Get out," she breathed. "Get out."

"Matt has tried twice to kill me," Jim said. "If you don't persuade him to leave the valley, I'll have to kill him. Or Troy will, and I don't want that to happen."

Mrs. Seery broke. She was not an aristocrat; she was not even a lady. She was a bitchy harridan. She lunged at Jim, cursing him with a muleskinner's vocabulary as she slapped him on one side of the cheek and then the other. Jim jumped back and wheeled and ran.

As he cleared the door, he saw Lily running down the hall toward him, a shotgun in her hands. He heard Mrs. Seery's hysterical scream, "Kill him, Lily! Kill him!" He plunged through the front door and across the porch, then stumbled on the steps and sprawled headlong on the grass as the shotgun blasted behind him, the buckshot sailing over his head.

Lily yelled, "Where does Matt keep his shells?"

He was on his feet and running again as he heard Mrs. Seery answer, "In his desk in the study." He ran through the gate in the fence, yanked the reins free from the hitch pole, and swung into leather before Lily appeared on the porch. He dug steel into his horse's flanks and rocketed down the street, wanting only to get out of Bakeoven.

He swung north across the grass, drawing a full breath of relief. He'd had something to be scared of, he thought, as he pulled his horse down to a walk. Only the accident of his tripping and falling had saved his life. He wondered what Jess Darket would have thought if Lily had blasted his head off. If Darket listened to Lily and Mrs. Seery when he got back, Jim would never get the deputy's badge.

Now that it was over, he could laugh about it. Troy would, too, when he told her. Jim Sullivan, who had shoved things around proper from the time he'd ridden into town, had come mighty close to getting himself killed by a crazy girl and a woman from whom he had snatched the mantle of goodness with which she had so carefully covered herself. And for what? Though he couldn't answer the question, he didn't think his visit with Mrs. Seery had been entirely futile. She had something to think about, something to nag Matt about, and it was possible she would get him out of the valley. Maybe that would be enough to satisfy Troy.

If Matt Seery stayed and retained the influence he had now, he could swing public opinion against Troy and anything she tried to do. As far as Pollock was concerned, Jim doubted that it would make any difference either way. Everyone in the valley except Matt Seery would be glad to see Pollock killed or driven away.

Jim crossed the creek fifty yards above where it flowed into the river, the water sluggish and heavy with silt. As he angled toward the north wall, he saw a herd of steers that was held in a large pasture to his right. Probably a pool herd that the small ranchers had thrown together for the drive to the railroad.

The north half of the valley was identical to what he had seen on the south side: good grass, land that sloped gently toward the creek, and a great sandstone wall rising above the valley floor. A man could get a stiff neck just sitting and looking at that rim. He had never seen anything like it until he had come to Rampart Valley.

He rode on, his thoughts turning to Troy. He wanted to marry her, to settle down at last. Here was a place where a man could live his life out and be content. In a way it was a miracle how his desires had changed. A combination of things had brought it about: the impact of the valley upon him, his dissatisfaction with his past, and most of all, the realization of how much Troy meant to him.

But he wasn't fooling himself about Troy. His future swung on her. He would ask her to marry him, and if she said No he'd ride out as soon as her troubles were settled. If she said Yes, well, what happened then depended on how firmly she clung to her nine-year-old passion for revenge.

He was halfway up the narrowing valley when he met a small herd being driven downstream, a cloud of red dust hanging above the cattle in the still air. He waved to the men riding point, and they waved back and went on. He turned toward the herd and motioned to one of the swing riders, who reined toward him.

"Looks like you're about ready to point 'em east," Jim called.

"Yeah, 'bout ready," the man agreed, pulling up. "This is the last bunch. Just drove 'em down from Marshal Mesa." He looked Jim over closely as if considering something, then he said: "If you're looking for a job, friend, you've got one. We're always short-handed this time of year on account of some of us have to get back on the mesa and round up our she-stuff."

Jim said: "No, I'm not looking for a job. You own a ranch hereabouts?"

The man nodded. "I'm Ben Yates." He jerked a thumb toward the creek. "That's my spread yonder. Circle Y."

"My name's Sullivan," Jim said. "I work for Troy Manders. She's bringing in a herd to stock her old place."

Yates' mouth was jarred open by that. He breathed: "Well, I'll be double damned. She know what she's up against?"

"She knows, all right." Jim shifted his weight in the saddle. "Yates, there's something I want to know. How would you and your neighbors feel about an irrigation system for the valley? Or at least a dam so you'd have plenty of stock water in a dry year."

Yates hesitated, a work-hardened hand wrapped around the horn. He was a big weather-burned man worn down by brush-popping until there wasn't an ounce of fat on him. He impressed Jim as unimaginative, but solid enough, the kind who could be depended on in a pinch.

"So Troy's got the same notion her dad had," Yates said finally. "Well, sir, it's just like it was when he was plugged. Nate Pollock don't cotton to the idea, and he'd block it. It's a good idea, and there's been many a year we needed it, but right now it just ain't practical."

Jim grinned at him. "That's what I wanted to know." He nodded at Yates and rode on, waving to the drag riders who were blanketed by the red dust rolling back from the herd.

He put his roan to a faster pace, wanting to see Troy. She'd be in her house by now. He wondered what had happened when she'd met Betty. Well, it was her business. He certainly wasn't going to raise a rumpus over Betty Erdman.

Presently he reached the upper end of the valley, the road making a turn to the south in front of Seery's ranch. He saw no sign of life there, and he wondered what Seery would do, now that his beef herd had been scattered and his men killed. He remembered how Troy had looked when Seery had told her what had happened. She would never forgive herself for sending the Dykens boys up there. Nothing had worked the way she had planned.

Jim was almost to the bridge spanning the creek when he saw the horses racked in front of Troy's house. He recognized Pollock's sorrel and Ace Rush's mount. He wasn't sure of the third horse, but he thought it was Bert Knoll's. Instinctively he reined off the road, and stopping behind the willows, pulled his Winchester from the boot and dismounted.

He had no idea what had happened, but Troy and Betty must be in the house. The crew hadn't got here yet. It was trouble, the worst trouble he could think of, and he was sick when he thought of what might be happening.

He waded across the stream to the willows that lined the south bank, and waited, peering through the leaves at the house. Then he heard a woman scream, a high, terrifying sound. Betty's voice! He dropped his Winchester, and ramming his way through the willows, sprinted toward the house, drawing his sixgun as he ran.

CHAPTER EIGHTEEN

The ground between the Manders house and the creek was flat and without cover except for the tall grass. If any of the three men inside the house saw Jim, he'd be a dead man, but the cold, calculating streak of caution that had brought him through so many tight squeezes was not controlling him now. He did not think of anything except that Troy and Betty were in trouble, and he blamed himself for loitering on his way from town.

Ace Rush came out of the house just as Jim cleared the corner. He had Betty Erdman in his arms, a kicking, clawing wildcat, and he was cursing her and threatening to kick her teeth in if she didn't behave. He saw Jim the same instant Jim saw him. He dropped the girl and grabbed for his gun, yelling, "Nate!"

If Rush had used the girl for a shield, he might have got Jim, but he was excited and furious. And hurt, too, for his face was lined with scarlet streaks that Betty's fingernails had given him. All he could think of was getting his gun into action, but a thin margin of time was against him. He never got his Colt clear of leather. Jim's bullet caught him in the left eye, and he was dead before he fell, spilling forward across Betty.

The whole thing was a swift explosion of action, breaking like a flash of lightning that leaves a man no chance to dodge or duck or plan. Bert Knoll stood in the doorway, stunned by Jim's sudden appearance. Betty, pinned under Rush's body, was screaming hysterically, the echoes of Jim's first shot dying in fading waves of sound.

Jim did not pause when Rush fell, but came on toward Knoll in long running strides as the man drew his gun and fired, a wild shot because Jim threw two slugs at the man that scored. Knoll toppled off the porch, a convulsive twitch pulling the trigger again, the bullet ripping into the first step. He went on down. Jim hurdled his body, hit the porch with both feet, and lunged on into the house.

Pollock's great bulk seemed to fill the room. He was laughing as he had laughed at danger all his life. He had an advantage of time that neither Rush nor Knoll had held: his gun was palmed, and he fired the second Jim was framed in the doorway.

The bullet splintered the jamb at Jim's side, a clean miss. Jim's shot broke Pollock's right arm. He lost his gun, but he was carrying two, and now he reached for the second with his left hand, a swift movement for a man as ponderous as he was. Jim, using his last bullet, shot him in the stomach.

As Pollock bent forward, Jim realized why the man had missed. Troy lay on the floor behind him, a smear of blood on her cheek from a cut just below her right eye. She had kicked him on the calf of his right leg, not much of a kick, but timed perfectly so that it ruined his aim.

Jim threw his gun down. Pollock was still on his feet, somehow holding his body upright like a bear that has been fatally wounded but still clings to a spark of life. He started lumbering toward Jim, left hand pulling a long-bladed knife from his belt.

Troy screamed: "My rifle. Beside you, Jim!"

There was no time to look for it. Jim bent low and lunged forward, Pollock's swinging blade missing by inches. Jim butted Pollock in the belly and knocked him down as Troy rolled and scrambled to her feet. Pollock's knife had fallen to the floor. Frantically he reached for the gun he had dropped and wrapped his fingers around it as Jim fell on him.

Troy, her rifle in her hands, shouted, "Get away, Jim! Get *away!*"

But Jim, not knowing she had the Winchester, got both hands on the barrel of Pollock's gun and twisted it from the big man's grip. He rose and moved back, only then aware that Troy was about to fire. He threw a hand out, knocking the rifle aside, shouting, "Hold it, Troy."

Pollock lay on his back, his pale eyes filmed by death. He made no effort to draw his other gun that was still in its holster, but he found strength to laugh. Jim, watching, could not keep from admiring a man who laughed while he died.

"You're a tough hand, Red," Pollock gasped. "You'n me, we should have been together."

Then he was dead, the smile still clinging to the corners of his mouth. Outside, a thunder of hoofs sounded south of the house. Troy ran outside, Jim a step behind her. Troy threw her rifle to her shoulder and fired, but missed, and the rider reached the aspens and disappeared.

Betty, trying to free herself of Rush's body, was still screaming, a shrill wave of wordless sound. Jim rolled the dead man off her. She jumped up and started to run. Jim caught her, spun her around, and slapped her sharply on the cheek.

"It's all right, Betty," he said. "It's all right now. You hear?"

The words got through to her. She stopped screaming, her mouth still open, her eyes wide and glazed with terror. He picked her up, and carrying her inside the house, laid her on the leather couch. Troy had dropped into a chair, the rifle on the floor beside her.

Jim dragged Pollock's body out of the house. He was too heavy to carry, and it was all Jim could do to drag him across the yard. He returned for Knoll, then Rush, and finding a canvas, covered them. He'd go to town and tell Ed Maylor. The undertaker would have to send a wagon for them.

When he returned to the house, he found that Betty was no longer hysterical but that Troy still sat in the chair, her head down, rocking back and forth, the chair creaking with the movement. Jim picked up his gun, reloaded, and dropped it into the holster. He bent over Troy and took her hands.

"You're all right, Troy; you're all right," he said. "Pollock's dead."

She looked up, her face filled with misery.

"You say I'm all right," she breathed, "but you're wrong, Jim. I'll never be all right. I can't forget the men the Dykens boys killed. I did it, Jim. I did it."

"That's crazy talk," Betty cried.

Jim pulled up a chair and sat beside Troy. He said: "Betty's right. I heard the orders you gave them."

"You told me I'd have to fire Gabe and his brothers," Troy said in a flat, expressionless voice. "I should have. That's what's wrong, Jim. I knew all the time what they were, but I thought I needed them, and now . . ." Her voice trailed off and she looked away. "I guess I've been a little crazy. I knew all the time I was wrong; down inside me I knew."

"Listen, Troy," Jim said softly. "You can't go back, so there's no sense driving yourself crazy with regret. You can go ahead. That's what counts, the things you do from here on out."

She tried to smile, but she couldn't. She said: "You're good, Jim. I wish I'd listened to you."

"I'm not very good." He rose, suddenly restless. "What happened here?" When she didn't answer, he added, "It'll wait if you don't feel like talking."

Troy made a quick, nervous gesture. "I'd

rather tell it now. We saw Pollock and the other two ride up. We were waiting for them. I said I'd kill them if they came in. They stood out there in front. Pollock laughed." She shuddered and looked away. "I'd forgotten how much he laughed. And the kind of things he laughed at. He laughed while my father died. I heard him before I was knocked out."

She couldn't go on. She started to rock again. Betty said: "Pollock told us we couldn't stay here. We weren't paying any attention to the back of the house. I thought the rest of his crew was on the mountain rounding up his beef herd, but a Mexican boy who works for him came in the back and got his gun on us. Pollock and his men came in. He got mean. He said folks thought I was his woman, and from now on I was going to be. He hit Troy and knocked her down, and Rush picked me up and carried me outside. That was when you came."

Betty must have screamed when Pollock knocked Troy down, Jim thought. He said: "The fellow who got away. Was he the Mexican boy?"

"Yes," Troy said. "He'll get the rest of Pollock's crew and they'll be back. They'll kill us, Jim."

He shook his head. "Pollock's been the

big gun. Now that he's dead, his bunch will break up. Chances are, they'll drive his beef herd into Utah and sell them. Our troubles are over, Troy."

But there was still Matt Seery. Jim didn't want to mention him, and apparently Troy didn't, either. She'd had enough of killing. If Seery would let her alone, Jim thought, she'd forget her resolve to make Seery crawl out of the valley on his belly. But would he let her alone? And what about Betty?

Jim paced the room, deciding there was no pressing danger. Seery was a man who would use others like Pollock. At this moment Seery stood alone. Still, the man was a schemer, and he had courage in his own peculiar way. Jim could not be sure about him.

"No, our trouble isn't over, Jim," Troy said finally. "That's what worries me. I'm to blame, and nothing you can say will make it any different."

She told him about Gabe Dykens's visit and his threat to kill Jim. She finished with: "Gabe will stay around, Jim. I knew how he felt about me, but I'd always been able to handle him. I was always able to handle anything until I got back here, and now . . ." She licked her lips and clenched her fists. "I couldn't stand it if he killed you, Jim. I just couldn't stand it."

"I'll take care of him. It's been coming for a long time." He rolled a cigarette, thinking that Moloch killing Seery's men was typical of him. He added: "It's too bad Molly plugged Enoch. He was the only one of the three who was worth a damn."

"I never saw Gabe like he was when he came here," Troy said. "It seemed like everything good in him had been destroyed."

"Maybe it had. Maybe whatever good he had he got from Enoch." He turned to Betty. "What are you going to do?"

"I'm leaving," she answered. "I'd like to catch the stage tonight."

"I've asked her to stay," Troy said.

Betty rose. She looked at Troy, fighting to hold back her tears, and Jim, watching, saw a warmth of feeling in her thin face that he had not seen there before.

"It's a wonderful thing to meet someone like you," Betty whispered, "after being dragged through the muck the way I've been, but if I stayed some of the muck would get on you. I can't do it."

Troy rose, her head high, a hint of her old spirit in her. She said: "Betty, I don't give a damn about the muck. If that's the only reason you —"

"No, there's another one," Betty said. "As long as I stayed here, I'd be reminded of what I've been by the way people looked at me every time I went to town."

She was thinking of Seery, too, Jim thought. If she stayed out here, Seery would find a way to strike at Troy. Jim said: "I'll take her to town. The boys'll be here before long. You'll be all right."

"I'm not afraid," Troy said.

"I'll get my horse and saddle yours for Betty to ride," Jim said. "You take what you need, Betty. We'll send the rest of your things to you if you'll let us know where you are."

"I'll let you know," Betty said, her eyes on Troy. "I want you to come to see me. You could never know how much it would mean to me."

Jim left the room. He glanced back as he went through the door and saw that Troy had her arms around Betty and that Betty was crying. A strange thing, he thought, the strangest thing he had ever seen. Now, after nine years, Troy felt the need of a woman's friendship, and the queer part of it was that the woman was Betty Erdman.

CHAPTER NINETEEN

Matt Seery did not tarry at Pollock's ranch after Rafael Tafoya rode in, babbling about Nate Pollock being shot. Ace Rush and Bert Knoll, too. It was fantastic, unbelievable that all three were dead at Jim Sullivan's hand, yet he did not doubt Tafoya's story.

"You'd better ride up the mountain and tell the boys," Seery said.

He mounted and rode toward town, not waiting to see whether Tafoya obeyed. His thoughts were in a turmoil. Nate Pollock was dead. Troy Manders had succeeded in exacting half the revenge she wanted.

Dust from the slowly approaching herd rose directly ahead of him. He glanced back toward the Triangle M, half expecting to see Sullivan coming after him, but no one was in sight. He had completely forgotten his plan of getting out of the valley with Betty. Town offered a sanctuary. He would be safe in his study. Or in the bank where the Seery cloak of respectability would cover him.

He swung off the road toward the creek, wanting to have nothing to do with Troy Manders' crew. When he was past them, he turned back to the road and went on to town. Now, recovering from the shock of Pollock's death, he began to recast his plans.

Troy Manders wouldn't send Sullivan to town to kill him. He was reasonably sure of that. They might strike at him by spreading gossip about him and Betty, but all he had to do was to deny it. His mother's position in the valley would protect him. His own position, too. No one had ever questioned his morals.

Now, with a sort of feverish frenzy, he kept telling himself that he was well rid of Pollock. The shadowy life he had lived was gone. He could not bring himself to think of Betty. She was part of the shadowy life. The respectable life, the Seery life, was the one that gave him security. He'd sell his ranch. He'd devote his time to the bank and the stage-and-freight business. He'd marry Lily just as his mother wanted. He'd have Jess Darket on his side, too.

Only a small arc of the sun was showing when he reached town and led his horse into the barn. He rubbed the animal down, finding satisfaction in the simple task. He could not rid himself entirely of the sick emptiness that clung to his belly. He had reasoned himself into reversing his plans, into accepting a life he had been intent on throwing away only a few hours before.

But something was wrong. He lingered in the barn while the light grew dim, until all things seemed weird and unreal and not in proper proportion. He smoked his pipe and found comfort in it. Thinking clearly now, he realized it was Betty's loss that had made him a little crazy. She was with Troy Manders and Jim Sullivan, and therefore she was probably out of his life forever.

He didn't know what to do about it. He paced along the runway, thinking of his cowhands who had been murdered. Of Perkins. Of Pollock and Knoll and Rush. He clenched his fists and sweat ran down his face. Troy Manders would get at him somehow. He didn't know how, but she would. If Sullivan was dead . . . He was her strength, her right arm.

The way Tafoya had told it, Sullivan was hell on tall red wheels. But a tough hand like Sullivan could be killed. Seery should have done it the afternoon they'd looked at the dam site. Or he should have let Pollock and his boys knock him out of the saddle when they were on their way back to town.

Those opportunities were gone, but there would be others.

He suddenly realized he was hungry; he might just as well go into the house and face his mother. She'd sense that something had happened and she'd put him on the rack with her questions, but he'd have to evade them. He left the barn, moving rapidly through the darkening twilight to the kitchen door.

A lighted lamp was on the table when he went in, and he saw that his meal was set out for him. A fire was burning in the stove, the coffee still hot. He took off his hat and coat and poured the coffee. Someone came in from the dining room and closed the door. He thought it was his mother, but when he looked up he saw it was Lily. He went to her at once, not wanting her to know how completely his world had tumbled in upon him.

She asked, her body stiffly erect, "Where have you been?"

"At the ranch," he said, and kissed her.

She didn't return his kiss. When he stepped back, she remained motionless, staring at him, her face pale. She had never been that way before. He returned to the table, telling himself that of all the people who lived in Rampart Valley, Lily was the last one he should worry about.

"Have a cup of coffee with me," he said.

"No." She took a long breath, her hands fluttering uncertainly at her sides. "Matthew, two men are in the front room. They want to see you."

He stood behind his chair, panic threatening to break him. He asked hoarsely, "Who are they?"

"I don't know, but go see them and get them out of here. I'm afraid of them."

Strangers! Probably Troy Manders' men. Then the panic died. Even if the Manders woman had sent them, they wouldn't kill him in his house. Besides, his gun was in his pocket. He asked, "Where's Mother?"

She glanced away. "I don't know."

He walked down the hall, wondering about his mother. She was probably at the church. He wasn't sure, but it seemed to him she had said something about a Ladies' Aid dinner. He opened the door into the front room and went in. The big hobnail lamp on the mahogany table threw a shaded light around it. Two men had been sitting on the couch. They were on their feet now, one of them moving toward him, asking, "You Matt Seery?"

"That's right," Seery answered.

They were strangers, cowhands, the

toughest-appearing men he had ever seen. His right hand in his pocket gripped his gun. The man who stood in front of him looked him over, judging him. He was tall and lantern-jawed with long ears and a lean hard face. His eyes were pale blue. Killer's eyes, Seery thought.

He had seen the kind. Not men like Jim Sullivan. Or Bert Knoll who had been able to live in a community for years and obey orders and stay reasonably clear of trouble. This fellow was ruled by some secret, dark passion, a man like the ones Seery had helped dodge the law by guiding them to safety across the state line. But he did not feel that the stranger disliked him. He was simply measuring him with his eyes, weighing him before he said why he was there.

"I'm Gabe Dykens," the man said finally. "This is my brother, Molly."

Seery glanced at the other man and nodded. They were entirely different. Molly had an oversized head and a stupid grin that seemed glued on his lips. The tip of his tongue was lodged where his upper front teeth should have been. He said, "Howdy," and kept on grinning.

The fellow was a half-wit, but there was nothing half-witted about the man called Gabe. His pale eyes were wicked but intelligent, and they kept boring into Seery, who fought an urge to back out of the room and run. The wickedness plainly dominated the intelligence.

"I've got a proposition," Gabe Dykens said. "Our guns are for sale, and we figured you were in the market to buy." He paused, letting his words have their effect, then added, "To kill Jim Sullivan."

That jolted Seery. They weren't from the Manders woman after all. Not unless this was some kind of trap. When Seery didn't say anything, Gabe went on, "While Molly and me was hanging around the saloon, we picked up some talk about how Sullivan has been raising hell since he hit this country. Molly and me need money and you need a man killed. Seemed like we oughta get together."

"What gives you the idea I'd hire a man to kill Sullivan?" Seery asked.

Gabe gave him a cold smile. "I knew Troy Manders in No Man's Land where she had a ranch, and I knew she was coming here to get you and a gent named Pollock. Well, Molly and me don't like Sullivan, but we ain't beefing him just for fun. Too much risk in a country we don't know. On the other hand, if you make it worth while, we'll do the job and light a shuck out of the country."

He could be on the level, Seery decided. People like Troy Manders and Jim Sullivan made enemies. These men might have followed them, finally catching them here in Rampart Valley. "I see," Seery murmured, "but you didn't pick up some talk in the saloon like you said."

"We picked it up, all right," Gabe said. "About Sullivan killing one of Pollock's men and winging another one. But we knew before we got here what the Manders woman and Sullivan aimed to do. It's like I said. We've got our own bone to pick with 'em, only it ain't a big enough bone to risk getting our necks stretched unless we was paid to take the risk. Say, a thousand dollars."

Seery was silent for a moment. He had nothing to lose. If this Dykens fellow tried to shift the blame to him, he would deny it and that would be the end of it. On the other hand, a thousand dollars would be a cheap price to pay for Sullivan's death.

"It's a deal," Seery said, "but I don't have that much cash on me. I'll get it from the bank later tonight. Sullivan isn't in town anyhow. He's at the Manders place."

Gabe shrugged. "You can give us half tonight, the rest after we plug him. That fair?"

"Fair enough," Seery said. "Make it an hour, behind the livery stable."

Gabe nodded. He motioned to his brother, and they walked out of the house. Seery stood motionless for a moment, pleased with himself. His luck was running high again. With Sullivan out of the way, he didn't have a thing to worry about. If these men failed, he'd have to figure out a way to do the job himself. If they succeeded, well, that would solve a good many things. He might even find a way to get Betty back.

When he returned to the kitchen, he found Lily standing where he had left her. He said, "My coffee's cold."

She took his cup to the sink and emptied it, then filled it with hot coffee from the pot. She brought it to him and walked back to the stove. He ate, not looking up, but feeling her steady stare. Hell, he couldn't marry her. Nothing could be worse than waking up after his wedding and finding himself in bed with her.

He rose, suddenly driven by a desire to get away from her. She said, "There's pie in the pantry."

"I'm not hungry," he said, and put on his coat.

"What did those men want?"

"Nothing," he said harshly, and started

toward the hall.

"Matthew."

The strained quality of her voice brought him around. She stared at him, a crazy wild temper in her. He had never seen her look at him this way, as if she hated and despised him. He said uneasily, "Well?"

"Why did you ever ask me to marry you? Why didn't you tell me you were living with that Erdman woman all this time?"

"Who told you that?" he shouted.

"Sullivan was here today. He told your mother. He said you'd been working with Pollock. It will come out now, Matthew. Don't you know what you've done to your mother? And me?"

Sullivan again! Seery labored with his breathing for a moment, the familiar weakness of panic threatening him. If Lily believed it, his mother must, too. His denial would not be enough. But because there was nothing else he could do, he said hoarsely, "It's a lie," and grabbing up his hat, stalked out.

He left the house and walked toward Main Street, the night air cold and heavy with the promise of rain. He shivered, finding it hard to believe that his mother and Lily would accept anything Sullivan said. But Vance Frane hated him. If Frane had discovered that Pollock's notes were missing, he'd prove what Sullivan had said.

That must be it, Seery thought. When his mother returned to the house, she'd have it out with him, and there wasn't a damned thing he could say that would convince her Sullivan had lied. She knew now she had not dominated him as she had thought, and she would hate him just as she had hated his father. She might even kill him. The possibility shocked him; but it shouldn't, he thought, for he had lived twelve years with the suspicion that she had murdered his father.

His position was untenable. He couldn't stay. He had reversed himself more than once in the last few hours, trying to decide what to do, hoping to salvage something from a life that had suddenly fallen apart. Now his mind was made up for him. If he had to leave, he might just as well clean out the bank safe. He knew Telescope Mountain as well as any man. He'd pick up some grub at Pollock's ranch, and a pack horse, and he'd disappear.

He was on Main Street before he realized it. The stage was waiting in front of the office. He stopped, his heart pounding. Betty was standing in the lighted area in front of the office, a valise at her feet, and she was talking to Sullivan.

At the moment Sullivan wasn't important. He'd be taken care of. But if Betty left, he'd never know where she went; he'd never see her again. If she knew what he was going to do, knew that he would give her the things he had denied her, it would be all right.

He broke into a run. He felt no panic now, only a hard, cold purpose. He didn't care what he lost if he could have Betty. His past mistakes with her ran through his mind. He wouldn't make them again. If he salvaged nothing out of all this failure but Betty, he would still have a good life.

She heard him running toward her and swung away from Sullivan, who stepped to one side, hand on a gun butt. Seery didn't look at Sullivan; he wanted no trouble with him now. He stopped a step from Betty, breathing hard, his eyes on her thin face; and even at that moment he noted that the light from the stage office touched her hair and turned it red-gold.

She said, "Let me alone, Matt. Don't touch me. Don't try to stop me."

"I'm not trying to stop you," he said, struggling for breath. "Listen to me, Betty. Just listen. I want to marry you. I love you. I wouldn't be here talking to you if I didn't. You believe me, don't you?"

"Seery —" Sullivan began ominously.

Betty wheeled on him. "Stay out of this." She turned again to Seery. "I'd like to believe you, Matt. I've always wanted to believe you."

He saw a tenderness in her face he had not seen for a long time. Suddenly it came to him that the simple act of standing on Bakeoven's Main Street in front of everyone and talking to her was the vital thing he had refused to do, that his refusal had been the reason she had turned away from him.

"I'm leaving Bakeoven," Seery said in a low tone. "I can't go with you on the stage, but I'll find you if you tell me where you're going. I'll find you and marry you. We'll have the kind of life you've always wanted."

"Let her alone, Seery," Sullivan grated. "Haven't you done enough to —"

Betty silenced him with a gesture. She moved to Seery and put her hands on his arms. "I'll wait in the county seat," she said. "Kiss me, Matt."

He kissed her, his arms tight around her, vaguely aware that the driver had climbed to the high seat. A man on the ground called, "Roll 'em."

"You going, Betty?" Sullivan demanded.

She pushed Seery away, giving Sullivan a faint smile of triumph, and got into the stage. The silk swept out and cracked sharply; the horses lunged forward and the wheels rolled and dust rose and drifted toward Seery. She wasn't running away from him tonight, he thought. She'd wait for him. He'd find her. It was going to be all right after all.

Jess Darket drifted out of the shadows. He stood in front of Seery, a shorter man who had to tip his head back to look at him. Darket's face was filled with contempt. He said hoarsely: "By God, Matt, I didn't believe it! Sullivan told me, and I called him a liar."

It was then that Seery saw the star on Sullivan's shirt. He was the law. Darket had done it. But it didn't make any difference. Gabe Dykens and his brother would get Sullivan. In any case, Seery would be out of town and in the mountains before Sullivan found out he had robbed the bank.

He walked swiftly down the side street to the alley head and turned into it. The sooner he got out of town, the better. He had a key to the back door that led into his private office, but he decided against using it. It would be better to break in through a window. The Dykens men were strangers, probably wanted men. They would naturally be suspected when the robbery was discovered, and Sullivan would go after them, giving Seery several days' start before anyone thought of him.

He edged along the side of the building until he reached a window. He found a rock and paused a moment to listen. No sound. Carefully he aimed, smashed a pane of glass, then reached inside and released the lock. He raised the sash and crawled into the building. Again he paused, eyes searching the darkness. He could make out nothing suspicious. He felt his heart pound, felt the drum of a pulse in his temples. Hell, he was boogery, he thought.

For a moment his caution got the best of him. Maybe he was crazy to risk this when he had enough money in the county seat to get along. . . . A noise in the back of the room startled him. He yanked his gun out of his pocket and wheeled. He caught a hint of movement and fired, then a ribbon of flame lashed out toward him and he fell back against the wall and his feet slid out from under him. The gun hammered out again and again, bullets searching for him as they slapped into the wall. He felt as if a great club had struck him in the chest, and he knew he was dying.

Dimly he heard Vance Frane scream, "You dirty bastard, you shot your mother!"

Someone was smashing the front door open. A lamp came to life as men poured in from the street. Seery thought of Betty, who would be waiting for him at the county seat, but he would never come to her. That was the only regret in him as he died.

CHAPTER TWENTY

Jim felt genuine sympathy for Jess Darket as he stood beside him at the bar in the saloon. Darket had been hit hard by the truth that he had called a lie only a short time before. He had not gone to the county seat. He had wired from Placerville and the sheriff had wired back, telling Darket that Jim could have a deputy's badge, and promising that the appointment would be confirmed by mail.

Darket, returning to Bakeoven sooner than he had expected, had found Jim in the livery stable and Jim had told him what had happened and the part Seery had played in the whole business. Darket, indignant and angry, had called him a liar. But the meeting between Seery and Betty beside the stage had been proof enough of what Jim had said.

They had been here for an hour, not drinking, just staring at the mahogany or at each other. Jim knew how it was with Darket. You had faith in a man, and when that faith was shattered it was hard to believe in anyone or anything.

Darket said again, as he had said over and over, "My God, Sullivan, what will happen to Lily?"

"She's better off. You ought to think of it the other way. What if she'd married Seery?"

But Darket found no comfort in Jim's words. At such a time truth was bitter, too bitter to be watered down. Lily was all Darket had, her happiness the only important thing in the world to him. They waited in silence, not knowing how badly Mrs. Seery had been wounded.

"Good and evil," Darket said presently, talking more to himself than Jim. "God and the devil. Old man Manders used to talk about it. He said sometimes you couldn't tell one from the other a lot of the time, and some of us who thought we were worshiping God were worshiping the devil."

Jim said nothing, hoping Darket could find release by talking. But he was silent then, and Jim said: "It's Betty I don't savvy. You suppose she was really going to wait for him?" Darket made no answer. He didn't know and he cared less. Jim went on: "About the dam. I'm going to try to get

Troy to build it. She's got to put her mind on something different than she's had it on, and if she's going to stay here she's got to be a part of the valley."

Darket looked up. "Maybe that was what was wrong with Matt."

"I'm talking about Troy."

"I mean what you said about her being part of the valley. I can't quit thinking about Matt. His dad was a mean old devil, and his mother — hell, I don't know what Lily sees in her. But Matt was different from either one. He loved that chestnut gelding of his like a brother, and Lily says he had a kitten he was crazy about. But you know there wasn't a man in the valley who could be called a friend of his, a real friend."

Darket tapped on the bar with his fingertips, frowning as he thought about it. He went on: "Matt never came in here for a drink. Never played a game of poker in his life that I know of. I guess his mother wouldn't let him, and him a man grown."

Darket was probably right, Jim thought. Seery had lived in the valley all of his adult life, but if he hadn't had a friend he hadn't been accepted. Respected, bowed to, but not accepted. There was nothing quite so terrible as being with people and still living alone.

The batwings opened and swished shut. Jim swung around. The doctor had come in. Darket asked, "How is she?"

"Unless there's some complication," he answered, "she'll be all right. Lily's with her."

"Did you find out how Mrs. Seery happened to be in the bank with Frane when Matt showed up?" Darket asked.

The doctor said: "Frane told me after he calmed down. Sullivan had told her about Matt. She didn't believe it, but she went down to the bank to talk with him. He was gone, so she told Frane what Sullivan had said. Frane thought about looking for Pollock's notes. They were gone. She smelled a rat then. After Frane locked up, he went to Mrs. Seery's house, and he was still there when a couple of hardcases showed up asking for Matt."

"The Dykens boys?" Jim asked.

The doctor threw him a questioning glance. "Frane said that was their name. You know them?"

"I know them," Jim said. "Go on."

"Well, these men said they'd wait. Mrs. Seery and Frane were in the parlor when Matt talked to them but he didn't know they were there. Mrs. Seery heard him promise to pay them a thousand dollars to kill Sullivan."

Jim thought: Gabe wouldn't miss a chance to make a killing pay. So it wasn't over. He'd have to watch his back as long as they were alive. They'd dry gulch him as he rode along some lonely trail. That would be Moloch's way.

"Mrs. Seery knew Matt didn't have a thousand dollars," the medico went on. "He told them hardcases he'd get it from the bank, so when he went back to the kitchen to eat his supper Mrs. Seery and Frane hightailed down to the bank. He came in through a window, and Mrs. Seery started toward him. He shot her, not knowing who it was, I suppose, and Frane plugged him."

After the doctor left, Jim said: "I'd better be riding, Jess. I'll keep the deputy's badge, but maybe you can get Ed Maylor to take the marshal's star back. I won't be staying in town."

"Didn't figure you would." Darket walked out of the saloon with Jim, asking, "Who are these fellows, Dykens, or whatever their name is?"

"A couple of killers who are gunning for me," Jim said, and let it go at that.

They walked through the archway into the stable, Darket calling, "Bill." But the hostler didn't answer. Darket swore. "I'll fire that lazy son. He's got a bottle and crawled into the mow."

"What do I owe you for taking care of the horses?" Jim asked, stopping in the cone of light thrown downward by the lantern hanging overhead.

"Nothing," Darket said. "Hell, you'd better ask what we owe you."

Jim stepped to his saddle and reached for it, glancing at Darket's grave face. As long as he stayed in the valley, he would have at least one friend. In the short time he had been here, he had learned to like and respect Jess Darket, but it was not a thing he could put into words, so he only said, "Then maybe we're square."

"Sullivan!"

Gabe Dykens's voice! Jim froze, a hand on the saddle horn. He had not expected it to happen here. And he had brought Darket to his death. Gabe could not afford to let him live, knowing what had happened. Jim dropped his hand to his side and made a slow turn. Gabe must have been hiding in a stall. Now he stood in the runway, his legs spread, his weight balanced, right hand splayed over gun butt.

Gabe was not a man to take a chance. Moloch was around somewhere, maybe behind Jim. He was whipped, caught in the light as he was. He had no chance unless he located Moloch. He could not see Gabe's face clearly, but he sensed the hatred that was in the man, hatred that had smoldered for months and had now burst into open flame.

A horse in a back stall kicked at the partition, a crashing sound in the silence, and Darket called, "Stop it, Spike."

Jim wondered if Darket was scared, if he understood what was shaping. Gabe seemed to be in no hurry. He stood motionless, his lean head tipped forward a little, hat brim shading his eyes. He was like many killers Jim had known, squeezing out of the moment all the pleasure he could.

"Enoch said I'd have a fair draw," Jim said, "but Troy told me you let Molly kill Enoch. He was the best man of the three of you, Gabe."

Still Gabe didn't move, and he didn't say anything. Waiting. Maybe for Moloch, who might be outside. A prickle ran down Jim's spine, and sweat broke through the skin of his face. He thought briefly of Troy. At one time he had wondered if Troy would take his death as lightly as Betty Erdman had taken Bob Jarvis's, but now he was ashamed of the thought. He had to live, for Troy needed him; she would always need him.

"Where's Molly?" Jim shouted. "Damn it, Gabe, is he going to shoot me in the back?"

Gabe never answered. A shot roared behind Jim, as loud as thunder within the walls of the stable. An involuntary cry broke from Gabe, a wild, wordless sound, and his hand drove downward toward his gun and brought it up.

Jim made his draw. He had no time to look around, but he knew the play was not going the way Gabe wanted it. His gun swung up and came level, a swift, rhythmical movement; he fired and felt the solid buck of it in his hand.

Both explosions rolled out together; gunflame made its brief, bright rosette of flame and was gone. Smoke rose and spread in writhing clouds above the runway. Horses squealed and kicked at the partitions of their stalls, then silence fell as they became quiet, the smell of burned powder lingering in the stable.

Jim stood motionless, his gun in front of him, held hip high. He watched Gabe wilt, slowly at first, then break at every joint at once and fall on his face. Jim walked toward him, hearing Darket say, "I got the other one."

Jim didn't look around. He stood over Gabe as the man brought himself up on hands and knees with stubborn strength. He cursed Jim, blood running from the corners of his mouth, and his eyes were terrified with the knowledge that life was running out. Then his head sank, his elbows gave under his weight, and he settled face down into the barn litter.

When Jim holstered his gun and swung around, he saw Moloch's body in the archway. He had been outside, waiting. Something had gone wrong with Gabe's plan, but at the moment Jim could not guess what it had been. Darket pulled Moloch's body out of the way and turned.

"They'll get their thousand dollars in hell," Darket said, "if Matt's got an account there."

"I'm in your debt again," Jim said.

"No," Darket said. "We're even."

Men drifted cautiously in from the street, attracted by the gunfire. Jim saddled up, not wanting to talk, not wanting to answer questions. As far as the Bakeoven men would ever know, a couple of gunslingers who had been hired by Matt Seery to kill Jim Sullivan had made their try and failed, not knowing they wouldn't have been paid if they had succeeded.

Jim left town, leading the horse Betty had ridden. Overhead the clouds had broken apart and the sky was filled with star diamonds. To Jim's left the south wall was a dark mass crowding the valley. Probably it wouldn't rain for a while, Jim thought absently. Weather changed, but not the wall. It would be there a thousand years from now, perhaps with a few soft spots drilled out by the wind, but otherwise unchanged. Then, as he rode, peace of mind came to him, the peace that follows turbulence that is spent.

It was late when Jim reached the Triangle M and stripped gear from the horses, but there was a light in the house. He went toward it, walking fast, filled with what he had to tell Troy. He stopped in the doorway, surprised.

She had taken off her riding clothes and had put on a red robe that probably belonged to Betty. She was sitting in a rocking chair beside the table, sewing, piles of blue-flowered material all around her. It was the first time Jim had seen her sew.

She looked up, brown eyes bright with laughter. "Sit down before you fall down, Jim. I was hoping I'd get this finished before you got back because I wanted you to see me in a dress, but I'm glad you're here." He sat down, and her face grew grave as she sensed something had happened. She said,

"Tell me, Jim."

He told her about it, while she went on sewing, one side of her tanned face lighted by the lamp. When he finished, she said: "I'm glad it's over. I would have been afraid for you as long as Gabe was alive. Bringing them here was the only real mistake I made. It was like turning two mad dogs loose on the valley."

"I finally figured out what went wrong," Jim said. "Moloch didn't have sense enough to do any thinking for himself. Gabe was in the livery stable, knowing I'd come for the horses, and he had Moloch waiting outside so they'd get me in a cross fire. They'd tied the hostler up, but Gabe didn't figure on Darket coming in with me, and then he didn't know what to do. I guess he couldn't think of any way to keep Moloch from coming in. If he had, they'd have waited for another chance."

Troy nodded. "Funny about Gabe. Tough as he was, Molly was his weakness."

"And Betty was Seery's weakness," Jim said. "But I don't savvy her, telling him she'd wait."

"Jim, Jim," Troy murmured. "Betty said she hated him, and maybe she thought she did, but when he promised her in front of everyone that he would marry her she couldn't let him go."

There was silence, then, except for the squeak of her chair as she rocked. Finally she said: "It's a strange feeling, Jim, but now that I'm back it seems like my father is alive. I found his Bible and the diary he wrote in every night. He had a lot of notes about the dam, its size, and the tests he made and everything. I don't think it will be hard to build. We'll do it the way you wanted to, all of us sharing the water and the work. It's what he wanted, too."

She glanced at him and brought her eyes back to her sewing again. "It's not easy for me to say I've been wrong, but I'm saying it. Now that I'm back, I can see how important some things are that I didn't think were important, and the other way around."

When he didn't move, she went on: "I shouldn't have kissed you that night on the Dolores. A man has to take the lead in things like that. I won't change overnight, but I'm going to work on it."

"Maybe it's time I was taking the lead," he said.

He rose, and walking to her, gripped her hands and pulled her to her feet, the scissors and needle and cloth falling unnoticed from her lap. He put his arms around her and kissed her. She was fire in his arms;

hunger was alive in her, and she wanted him to know. And when she drew her lips from his, she breathed, "Tomorrow, Jim. Tomorrow."

She was a lot of woman, Troy Manders was.

ABOUT THE AUTHOR

Wayne D. Overholser has won three Golden Spur awards from the Western Writers of America and has a long list of fine Western titles to his credit. He was born in Pomeroy, Washington, and attended the University of Montana, University of Oregon, and the University of Southern California before becoming a public school teacher and principal in various Oregon communities. He began writing for Western pulp magazines in 1936 and within a couple of years was a regular contributor to Street & Smith's *Western Story* and Fiction House's *Lariat Story Magazine*. *Buckaroo's Code* (1948) was his first Western novel and remains one of his best. In the 1950s and 1960s, having retired from academic work to concentrate on writing, he would publish as many as four books a year under his own name or a pseudonym, most prominently as Joseph Wayne. *The Bitter Night, The Lone*

Deputy, and *The Violent Land* are among the finest of the early Overholser titles. He was asked by William MacLeod Raine, that dean among Western writers, to complete his last novel after Raine's death. Some of Overholser's most rewarding novels were actually collaborations with other Western writers: *Colorado Gold* with Chad Merriman and *Showdown at Stony Creek* with Lewis B. Patten. Overholser's Western novels, no matter under what name they have been published, are based on a solid knowledge of the history and customs of the American frontier West, particularly when set in his two favorite Western states, Oregon and Colorado. When it comes to his characters, he writes with skill, an uncommon sensitivity, and a consistently vivid and accurate vision of a way of life unique in human history.

We hope you have enjoyed this Large Print book. Other Thorndike, Wheeler, Kennebec, and Chivers Press Large Print books are available at your library or directly from the publishers.

For information about current and upcoming titles, please call or write, without obligation, to:

Publisher
Thorndike Press
295 Kennedy Memorial Drive
Waterville, ME 04901
Tel. (800) 223-1244

or visit our Web site at:

http://gale.cengage.com/thorndike

OR

Chivers Large Print
published by BBC Audiobooks Ltd
St James House, The Square
Lower Bristol Road
Bath BA2 3SB
England
Tel. +44(0) 800 136919
email: bbcaudiobooks@bbc.co.uk
www.bbcaudiobooks.co.uk

All our Large Print titles are designed for easy reading, and all our books are made to last.